Kelly was having never felt more relaxed or more responsive to the camera, and she knew these shots with Mickey were going to be among the best she'd done.

There was a feeling of excitement and recklessness in the air. Kelly felt every inch the slinky flapper, and if she hadn't known the "gin" in their glasses was only club soda, she would've sworn she was giddily drunk.

"I think you're having an effect on me," she told Mickey.

"You ain't seen nothing yet. . . ."

Kelly Blake
TEEN MODEL

One day she's an A student at Franklyn High with a major crush on the boy next door. Then she's discovered by the head of the prestigious FLASH! modelling agency. Almost overnight, Kelly becomes the hottest new face in the modelling world!

Each of the KELLY BLAKE titles features the ongoing characters and events in Kelly's life. While romance is part of that life, these books are more than romances; they deal with the experiences, conflicts, crises and behind-the-scenes details of modelling.

Ask your bookseller for the titles you have missed:

••••••••4••••••••
KELLY BLAKE
TEEN MODEL
••••••••••••••••••••••

Headliners

Yvonne Greene

BANTAM BOOKS
TORONTO • NEW YORK • LONDON • SYDNEY • AUCKLAND

With special thanks to
Abby Daniels, whose help
was invaluable.

RL 6, IL age 12 and up

HEADLINERS
A Bantam Book/July 1987

Setting of front cover photo courtesy of Wooster Gallery.

*Setting of back cover photo of Kelly Blake in the soda shoppe
courtesy of Antique Supermarket.*

ISBN 0-553-26112-6

Published simultaneously in the United States and Canada

Printed and bound in Great Britain by
Cox & Wyman Ltd., Reading

O   0 9 8 7 6 5 4 3 2 1

Headliners

One

"Friday afternoons are the pits!" Kelly Blake complained as she dug apple pie leftover from yesterday's Thanksgiving dinner out of the refrigerator. "Especially on holidays. They're like a warm-up for the rest of the weekend—perfect for worrying about not having a date Saturday night."

"Eric didn't ask you out yet?" Jennifer Lee, Kelly's best friend, let the forks and plates clatter onto the table. "What's wrong with that guy? That's no way to treat a girlfriend."

"I'm not his girlfriend," Kelly said. "He's still free to date Clarissa Robbins if he wants."

"That was a stupid thing to agree to," Jennifer said, sparing Kelly no pain. "You should've forced him to make a choice. Clarissa, or you."

"I know, but you try looking into Eric's blue eyes and giving him an ultimatum like that. What if he'd chosen Clarissa?"

"Then you'd be free to find an even better boyfriend," Jennifer said practically.

"Jen, you name one boy I could possibly like better than Eric Powers, and I'll take that risk."

"What about Alex Hawkins?"

"Of course not. Alex is really just a friend." Kelly was firm. "After everything I went through to get Eric interested in me, it would take a very special boy to make me forget him. A *very* special boy."

Jennifer slid a spatula into the pie plate and lifted out a huge slice.

"You never know. Stranger things have happened."

"Hi, girls." Kelly's mother entered the kitchen, balancing two heavy shopping bags. She dumped them onto the kitchen counter. "Can you believe that we needed all this food, when the refrigerator is packed with leftovers? But we can't eat turkey three times a day!"

"Hi, Mom. Here, I'll help you with those." Kelly stood up, and Jennifer followed her over to the counter.

Mrs. Blake pressed her hands into the small of her back. "Thanks, girls. Those groceries seem to get heavier all the time. That's a pretty outfit you're wearing, Jennifer. Kelly, why can't you wear pretty clothes like that? Jeans, jeans, jeans—don't you get tired of them?"

Here we go again! Kelly thought. "Mom, I like jeans. I look good in them. Hey, Jen, why don't you hand me the stuff and I'll put it away?"

Jennifer began to pull the groceries out of one of the bags. "Clothes like these aren't Kelly's style, Mrs. Blake. She's more of a—a free spirit than I am. In fact, I wish I felt comfortable in the things she wears. I wish I didn't have this compulsion to be well-coordinated all the time. It's dull, dull, dull."

"It's lovely and feminine." Mrs. Blake sighed. "My daughter, the tomboy."

"Your daughter, the model," Kelly reminded her. "The way I dress hasn't hurt my career, has it?"

"No, but that just shows that things aren't the way they were when I was a girl," her mother complained.

"Of course they're not. That's progress, Mom."

"Progress!"

Kelly put a bag of apples into the refrigerator. "Speaking of modeling, it's Friday afternoon and I've got to call my booker for my Monday assignment." She sat down by the telephone.

"Doesn't FLASH! have today off?" Jennifer asked.

"Yes, but Nina said she'd be in this afternoon to check the messages and see if any emergencies came up," Kelly explained as she dialed the agency's number.

Jennifer finished unpacking the bag, and Mrs.

Blake smiled at her. "Eat your pie, Jennifer. I'll finish these up."

"Nina? Hi, it's Kelly. What's up?" Kelly listened for a moment, then gave a loud cry, startling both her mother and Jennifer. A second later she hung up the phone and sprang to her feet, her curly brown hair bouncing on her shoulders.

"You won't believe this! I can't believe this is happening to me—I can't wait to go!"

"Go where?"

"What's happening?"

Kelly sank onto a kitchen chair. "You'll never guess what job Nina got me! Ten days on location—in the Greek Islands! Ten days on Corfu—can you believe it?"

"That's fantastic!" Jennifer cried. "That's the most exciting thing you've ever done."

"I know! Paisley Gregg is going, too, and the two of us will have so much fun! I think I'll buy a new bathing suit—nothing I have is right for a Greek Island. Oh, can you imagine the tan I'll get?"

"Hold on, Kelly," her mother warned. "Don't get so carried away. I'll have to discuss this with your father. He's upstairs."

"Dad's home? Well, great! I can't wait to tell him my big news."

"Yes, he's home. He's working a night shift today. But he might not be too excited about your news." Mrs. Blake poured herself a cup of coffee and sat down across from Kelly, her expression sober.

"Oh, Mom, don't look like that! Come on, you know I've got to go. This is a fabulous opportunity."

"I don't know how fabulous it is. Ten days on your own—I don't like the sound of it."

For the first time it dawned on Kelly that her mother might not be as thrilled as she was. "Mom, you're not going to tell me I can't go, are you? I'll die! Besides, I already said yes! Nina put me on the schedule."

"You shouldn't have said anything until you'd asked your father and me. First of all, when will this job be—during Christmas vacation?"

"No, it starts Monday."

"Monday! Well, now that's totally out of the question. You're not going to miss a week and a half of school, Kelly."

"But, Mom, this job is worth it. In the two months since I started modeling, I've never had an offer this big before! It's one thing to turn down a day job on a school day, but this is an important spread. And it's a free trip to Greece, and I've never been there—I've never been anywhere!"

"No arguments—there will be no decisions until I've heard all the facts. I'll call Meg Dorian at home and find out all the details."

"You don't need to call Meg," Kelly said in exasperation. As Kelly's booker, Nina handled most of her assignments for FLASH!, but Kelly's mother had become friendly with Meg Dorian, the head of the agency. "For crying out loud, don't you even think I'm capable of taking a phone message? I know the details; I wrote everything down."

She handed her mother the notepad she'd scribbled on. "That's the name of the hotel we'll be staying at, and this is the name of the airline and all the flight information."

"Fine." Mrs. Blake set the notepad aside on the table.

"In case you're interested, it's for *Jolie* magazine. You never even asked," she said bitterly.

"Watch your tone of voice, young lady."

"At least let *me* explain it to Dad. You're going to make it sound awful."

"I'm going to tell him the facts, that's all. He'll make up his own mind."

"Oh, sure. He'd never agree if you didn't. Come on, Jen. Let's go up to my room to wait for the verdict."

"Maybe I'd better go home," Jennifer suggested.

"Why? You've already heard the worst of it. If they're ashamed to tell me no in front of you, then they shouldn't be telling me no at all."

Kelly flounced out of the room. With an apologetic glance at Mrs. Blake, Jennifer followed.

"The island of Corfu. Doesn't it sound romantic?" Kelly asked.

"Yes," Jennifer said wistfully. "I wish I could go along as your assistant."

"That didn't work out too well, the one time we tried it," Kelly said wryly, remembering the disaster of her one and only television commercial. Jennifer's presence hadn't kept her from blowing her lines—and losing the job. "Anyway, I probably won't be going at all. My dad will never say yes."

"But isn't he more open-minded than your mother? Fathers have a much harder time saying no to their daughters."

"Not in this house, they don't."

There was a knock at the door, and Kelly's father, tall and striking in his police uniform, entered the room. "I guess we have something important to discuss. How are you, Jennifer?"

"Fine, thanks. Isn't Kelly's job offer exciting? I've always thought Greece was one of the most fascinating countries in the world."

Kelly shot her a grateful look.

"That may be," Kelly's father answered carefully, "but I'm not sure it's the place for Kelly. At least, not now, and not on her own."

"Dad, I thought we were going to discuss it! You've already made up your mind, just like Mom. You're dead set against this job, and for no good reason."

"It's not just another job, Kelly. It involves leaving school for more than a week, not to mention leaving the country. You're too young."

Kelly turned away. "Some career I'm going to have as a model—oh, Kelly Blake, don't call her for the job, her parents won't let her go," she said, mimicking her agent.

"That's not very fair," her father said sternly. "We've been very flexible about your other assignments, but this one's different."

"That's the point. . . . Of course it's different. This job's important! FLASH! really wanted it for me, and I've already said I could go, and now I have to call back and say my parents won't let me. They might never call me again—they'll think I'm a baby. Why did you and Mom ever let me sign a contract with FLASH! You shouldn't have if you were going to make me turn down every offer."

"We don't make you do that."

"No, not if a job is after school hours, or on a Saturday, which they hardly ever are."

"Kelly, you've never been anywhere alone, much less out of the country. You'll be very far from home, with no real chaperon."

"There will be a chaperon," Kelly said desperately. "An art director or an account executive— there's always someone there."

"Controlling a pack of young people who know their parents are thousands of miles away? I just don't see it, Kelly. Not for you. I'm sorry."

"Dad, you can't say no!" Her voice was husky with sudden tears. "It's so unfair. Paisley Gregg is going!"

"Your friend Paisley is older and more experienced than you."

"Of course she's more experienced. She hasn't been forbidden to go anywhere!"

"It's for your own good. Now, that's enough arguing. I'm sure Jennifer didn't come here to hear this."

"But what if . . ."

"No ifs. That's a final decision. You'd better call FLASH! and tell Nina you can't go after all." He gently laid a hand on her shoulder. "Sweetheart, there'll be other opportunities."

Kelly watched her father leave, then got up and shut the door behind him. "How could there ever be another opportunity like this," she cried bitterly. "It's just not fair."

"It's parents," Jennifer sympathized. "They're all alike. They don't realize that their darling little girls are nearly full-grown women, capable of running their own lives."

"What are they afraid of, anyway?" Kelly demanded. "Tell me one situation I couldn't handle. I'm not as young and naive as they think. They should know about some of the tough situations I've already handled in my life."

"Maybe they'd better not know," Jennifer said, and they both laughed.

Kelly sighed. "But this isn't funny, it's humiliating. How can I ever face Meg Dorian again?"

"You'll face her, because as long as we live at home, our parents control our lives."

"And with my parents," Kelly said, "I'll probably never get the chance to grow up."

* * *

After school on Monday, Kelly poured out her woes to the group of girls who crowded around her locker.

"I can't believe this! First I lose the Greece job, then I don't hear from Eric all weekend, and now I have to do my entire English paper over because Miss Paterson thinks I didn't understand the theme!"

"Losing that job was the worst thing," Lisa Daly said. "You must've been furious."

"I would've been more furious that Eric didn't call," their friend Rochelle Sherman argued.

"Not me," Jennifer said practically. "She can see Eric anytime, but a trip to Greece doesn't come along every day."

"Quiet!" Rochelle warned. "Here comes Eric now." She greeted him casually. "Long time no see. Have a good Thanksgiving, Eric?"

"Yeah, not too bad. How was yours?" He nodded at them all politely, adding a special smile for Kelly.

"Don't ask Kelly about her holiday," Rochelle warned. "She's in a terrible mood. Her parents made her refuse a modeling job in the Greek Islands. Can you believe it?"

"In *Greece*? Wow, parents can be a real pain sometimes," he agreed. "That's too bad, Kelly. I'm sorry I wasn't around to cheer you up."

"You're never around very much." She said it lightly, but she saw her friends exchange nervous glances. *Well, what do I care*, she thought defensively. It hurt to know Eric hadn't cared enough to let her know that he'd be busy for all four days of the holiday weekend.

"Sorry, my aunt and uncle's family came in from Ohio for the whole weekend. And right now I have to take my bike into the repair shop downtown," Eric explained. "There's something wrong with the brakes."

"Well, it was nice of you to stop to say hello," Kelly said grumpily.

"Kelly," Rochelle whispered, "lighten up. He said he was sorry." In a louder voice she said, "Come on, gang, let's get going. 'Bye, you guys."

Eric frowned after the girls had left. "Look, I don't plan to be so busy. There's just a lot of things I have to do."

"Sometimes," Kelly said, trying to keep her voice from quavering, "it might be nice if your plans included me."

Eric colored painfully. "We'll get together soon," he said quietly. "Are you going to be around this weekend?"

Kelly shrugged. "Where else would I be? I'm not allowed to go anywhere. The question is are you going to be around? Not back in Ohio?" She knew she was on dangerous ground, reminding Eric of the visit he'd paid to his old girlfriend not too long ago. In fact, she ought to be grateful that the Powerses hadn't gone back to Ohio for Thanksgiving. But she was finding it more and more difficult to believe that Eric would ever break up with Clarissa Robbins completely.

Eric's mouth drew into a grim line. "I was going to ask if you'd like to do something Saturday night, but maybe we'd better forget it until you're in a better mood." He turned and walked away.

Kelly hesitated, then ran to catch up. "Eric— I'm sorry. Really."

"What are you trying to do? Lay a guilt trip on me?"

"No."

"You could have fooled me."

"Eric, please, let's not quarrel. I'm just upset about this job and . . . well, I hardly ever see you these days. You can't blame me for being a little angry. You told me you wanted to see more of me. . . ."

"Kelly, I do. But does that give you the right to criticize me?"

"I don't know," she said miserably. "I didn't mean to take it out on you, but losing that job really upset me."

He glanced at his watch. "I've got to hustle or the bike shop will be closed. We'll get together Saturday night, okay?"

Kelly sighed. "Okay, Eric."

Kelly slammed the front door behind her, in a worse mood than when she'd left that morning.

Her mother heard the noise and hurried into the hall, smiling widely.

"Meg just called you. I took the message and said you'd call her right back."

"Why should I bother? It's probably another assignment I can't take." Kelly was almost afraid to hear what Meg would have to say, since she'd had to refuse the Greece trip. *What if it's another fabulous job I have to turn down? Or, worse, one that isn't up to the quality of the jobs I've been getting?*

Her mother raised her eyebrows. "Why don't you give it a try?"

"Well, all right," Kelly said reluctantly. "I'll call from my room."

Five minutes later Kelly found her mother in the kitchen. "It's a fabulous assignment," she said in a dazed tone. "Two days on location at a Long Island mansion, starting on Thursday, shooting a special fashion layout for *Couture*. There'll be celebrities there—including Mickey Pines!"

"So Meg told me," her mother said calmly. "But I didn't recognize the name."

"He's only one of the hottest new movie stars around," Kelly explained. "Mom, I've got to take this job. There's nothing wrong with it; it's close to home, and you can call me every hour on the hour if you want to! You've got to say yes to this one, it would be cruel to torture me this way."

"Perhaps," her mother said mildly. "I wasn't going to tell you this, but even Meg put on the pressure about this one. She said this assignment is a major break in your career."

"Then will you let me take it? Oh, Mom, please say I can go."

"Hold on, now. Your father and I feel very strongly about one thing. School always comes before modeling."

"Oh, school."

"That's right, school. You have a school career, too, and this job is during school hours."

Kelly felt a flood of disappointment. "Does that mean I can't take it?"

"I didn't say that. Actually, I agree with Meg about this job. It's a high-quality assignment, and it will be very good for your career."

Kelly stared at her mother, feeling a flicker of hope. "Then I can take it?"

"Since it's only for two days, yes. But before you go wild, there are strict conditions."

Kelly hugged her mother. "Thank you, thank you. I don't care what the conditions are! This is almost as good as going to Greece—just think, a movie star. I can't believe it!"

"Listen to me—you're to come right home after each day's shoot to do your homework. And if it's necessary, you'll sacrifice your social life to make up your missed classes."

"No problem! I can get all my assignments from friends, and I know I don't have any tests scheduled for Thursday or Friday. And I still have plenty of time to do my English paper over. Oh, Mom—I really can do it!"

"Yes. I guess it's all right to miss school this time, but I hope this isn't the beginning of a trend, Kelly. Sometimes I worry that modeling is taking over your life. You've already dropped out of track . . ."

"It's not taking over," Kelly said defensively. It *had* been very difficult lately to balance school and work commitments, but she was trying her hardest not to let modeling dominate. "It's just part of my life."

"I hope so. Then you agree to the terms? Schoolwork first."

"Of course! I'm not crazy enough to turn down a job like this. I promise, I'll make up all my work. Only, there is one thing . . ."

"No exceptions," Mrs. Blake said firmly.

"Just one, Mom—I have to keep my date with Eric Saturday night. I've hardly seen him at all lately."

"Oh, all right, Kelly! Keeping the date with Eric is fine if you keep up your end of the bargain."

"Mom, you're a doll! I love you." She raced to the closet in the hallway and grabbed her coat.

"Come back here," her mother called after her. "Where are you going?"

"To find Jennifer. I finally have some good news to tell her!"

Two

Kelly had just finished helping her sister Tina clear the table when the phone rang. "I'll get it," Kelly called. She ran to the other side of the kitchen, where the phone was. "It may be Meg with some last-minute details for the shoot tomorrow."

She picked up the phone with a flourish. "Hello," she said gaily.

"Hey there!" an exuberant male voice greeted her. "How's my favorite model doing?"

"Alex!" Kelly exclaimed with delight.

Tina dropped the dish towel on the kitchen counter and pranced around the room. "Ooooh, Mom—it's Alex," she crooned.

Kelly clamped a hand over the mouthpiece of the phone and glared at her younger sister. "Go away," she hissed. "Don't you have anything better to do than bother me?"

"Alex," she repeated, speaking into the phone once again. "How terrific to hear from you. What's up?"

"Well, I'm calling to tell you some great news." He paused and chuckled. "At least *I* think it's great."

"Well, tell me what it is!" Kelly urged him.

There was a dramatic pause before Alex spoke again. "Guess who's assisting Steve on this shoot tomorrow?"

"Alex—you're kidding. That's wonderful!" Kelly had worked with Steve Hollender, Alex's boss, several times before. He was, without doubt, one of the best photographers in the fashion business. But he could sometimes be short-tempered. Having Alex around, with his sense of fun, would lighten up the atmosphere and make the shoot perfect.

"I hoped you'd be pleased," Alex said.

"Of course I am," Kelly replied. "We always have so much fun working together." *And playing together, too*, she thought. *But I want to keep things light and friendly*, she reminded herself. *Alex is a terrific guy—and he sure knows how to take a girl out in style. But we're just friends— it's Eric I'm really interested in.* Yet no matter how often she told herself that, Kelly still felt very special in Alex's company.

"Alex—since this job's for *Couture*, you should get some great tear sheets for your portfolio."

"You bet. Hey, Kelly, listen, I was thinking. I know you'll probably be using a car service to get to the shoot tomorrow, which can be a real pain. So how would you like it if I picked you up early in the morning? We could drive to Long Island together. And, of course, I'd drive you back home after we're done."

"Alex, you're so sweet. Driving together would be fun. Just let me check with my mom."

Mrs. Blake was thrilled by the suggestion; she thought Alex was a delightful—not to mention good-looking—young man. She gladly gave Kelly her consent to drive with Alex, and invited him to have a late supper with Kelly on the next two nights.

Kelly gave her mother a quick hug. "Mom, you're the greatest," she called as she ran back to the phone.

"Alex, I'd love to drive with you—but only under one condition."

"Anything you want," Alex quickly replied, his voice showing concern.

"Mom says you've got to stay and have a late supper with me. It won't be what you're used to in New York, but . . ."

"I'd love to, Kelly!" Alex interrupted her. "I think these next two days are going to be the most fun I've had on a shoot in a long time!"

The wind blowing in off the ocean lifted Kelly's hair as she got out of Alex's car, but she barely noticed the cold.

"It's magnificent," she gasped, surveying the fabulous Long Island mansion called Windward Point. "I've never seen anything like it!"

"It's from the Roaring Twenties," Alex told her. "It's one of the most impressive estates on the South Shore."

"I'll say it's impressive. It's really going to be great working in a setting like this. I can't wait to see the inside."

"Let me go help unload the photographic gear, and I'll come back and give you a personal tour of the place."

"I don't think you'll have to." Kelly pointed at the wide front lawn. "It looks like Steve is giving his own tour." She took a deep breath. "I guess I'd better go meet the people I'll be working with."

"Don't look so terrified," Alex said, chuckling. "They won't bite. Celebrities are ordinary people inside, no different from you or me."

"Sure they are," Kelly said, rolling her eyes. But she didn't agree. As she marched toward the group of people gathered near the mansion's immense stone porch, she could feel her heart knocking against her ribs. Alex Hawkins might have grown up around the wealthy, the famous, and the powerful, but to Kelly Blake, celebrities were not ordinary people.

"Here's Kelly Blake," Steve said as Kelly hurried toward him, "one of our best new models. Kelly, let me introduce you to your new co-workers."

Kelly smiled agreeably as Steve introduced the

other two models, a willowy brunette named Maxi Bond and a pert blond named Cheri Lincoln. She shook hands with Lisa, a stylist whom Steve used occasionally, and Amy, the model editor for *Couture*. Kelly had worked with both women on her very first shoot, in Steve's studio. She nodded at everyone else as Steve named them: Marilyn Watson, the art director; Arlene Saccaro, the assistant art director; Pepe, the hairdresser; and Oliver, the makeup man.

"And these are the celebrated actors Sir Ernest and Lady Fiona Kendall," Steve said importantly, "and finally, we have Franklyn Deeds and Rebecca Halloway. Quite a glittering cast, wouldn't you say?"

"Oh, yes," Kelly said, blushing. "It's, well, really thrilling to work with all of you."

"The pleasure is mine," answered Sir Ernest in a clipped, aristocratic British accent. The tall, distinguished-looking actor reached for Kelly's hand. Before she realized his intention, he planted a kiss on it and bowed toward her.

"Oh, Sir Ernest, my mother will die when I tell her I've met you! She's seen all your movies, and once she even got to see you and Lady Kendall on the stage."

Sir Ernest frowned. "Your mother? Why, surely you've heard of me yourself, haven't you?"

"Oh—uh, of course," she stuttered, not wanting to offend Sir Ernest or his wife, Fiona.

Franklyn Deeds, famous for his rugged he-man roles, shook Kelly's hand limply and immediately turned toward Rebecca Halloway, the TV actress. "Tell me, Rebecca," he said, draping an arm around her waist possessively, "why haven't we met before?" He gave her an intimate squeeze, and Rebecca, tossing back her bleached blond hair, squealed in delight.

Kelly immediately decided Rebecca's true talent was in attracting men like Franklyn.

Steve glanced at his watch. "A quick tour and we'll be ready to begin shooting," he said, "but where in blazes is Mickey Pines? Arlene, is he coming soon?"

"I hope so," Arlene said. "I offered our limo but he insisted he'd arrange his own transportation."

Steve frowned. "As long as he understands what this shoot is all about. We can't have a prima donna on the set."

"He'll be here, I'm sure," Arlene said. "Wait—here comes a car now. That must be him."

Kelly felt her heart beat even more wildly. Mickey Pines, about to appear in person! *He's only human.* She tried to concentrate on Alex's words, but they made no impression. Every girl in Franklyn, New Jersey, was green with envy at Kelly's good luck. They were all awestruck, even her little sister, Tina, who usually disdained silly crushes on movie stars.

"I'm sure the real-life Mickey Pines is nothing like his movies," Kelly'd told Tina calmly. "That bad-boy-with-the-heart-of-gold image is only a role. He's probably not like that at all." But she hadn't really believed that.

As footsteps approached behind her now, she closed her eyes and took a few deep breaths to calm herself. She heard everyone else being introduced.

"And last but not least, this is our third model, Kelly Blake. Kelly, meet Mickey Pines."

Her heart in her throat, she turned around. "Hello," she stuttered.

A cloud of foul smoke blew in her face.

"Hrmmmph," a baby-faced boy grunted.

"Uh, it's . . . nice to meet you," she managed to say, choking back the cigarette smoke.

Dirty hair fell over eyes that didn't bother to look at her as he answered. "Yeah, sure," he grunted, ignoring her outstretched hand.

Kelly tried not to stare. *Is this the heartthrob I've read so much about?* she thought. Mickey rubbed a grubby fist into his eye and yawned in her face.

Steve, apparently not put off by bad manners, put a friendly arm around Mickey's shoulders. "Glad you're here, Mickey. You're in time for a little tour of Windward Point."

"Umm, great." He yawned again. "Sorry. I haven't had much sleep lately."

"That's fine, fine, " Steve murmured.

Maxi Bond tilted her striking head back, shading her eyes against the strong morning sun. Kelly noticed what a flattering pose it was.

"What's that supposed to be?" Maxi pointed to a large, glass-covered dome that dominated the west wing.

Steve squinted into the sun. "Ah—the observatory. We're going to do a special shot up there—as if you were having an intimate party to view the stars."

"Which stars," Maxi quipped, "the stars in the sky or the ones right here?" She batted her eyelashes flirtatiously.

Steve ignored her. "I'm trying to explain that I've planned special shots in almost every room of Windward Point—exactly what *Couture* wanted. And what the art director ordered." He nodded at Marilyn Watson.

"And don't think I won't get a full day's work out of all of you," Marilyn warned. Her sweeping gaze included everyone but the celebrities.

"Oh, but I think this job will be a pleasure," Cheri said, running her fingers through her hair and glancing at Mickey Pines.

"Don't count on it," Alex muttered to Kelly. "But I hope we'll have some free time. I'd like to get some shots of my own in—this setting is spectacular in the fall."

Kelly agreed. "I guess you could spend days taking pictures here."

"If he does, he'll be out of a job as my assistant," Steve barked at them.

Kelly flushed. Everyone in the group stared at them as if she and Alex were naughty children. She was especially uncomfortable since, at sixteen, she was the youngest person there.

She and Alex lagged behind the rest of the group as the tour began.

"Some terrific beginning," he said. "Steve is in his usual wonderful mood. He can be a royal pain."

"I hate it when Steve gets like this," Kelly agreed, "but let's stay on his good side. I've done my best jobs with him—for *Couture*, and *Jolie*, and some really good catalog spreads. He deserves his reputation."

"And don't think he doesn't know it," Alex said darkly. "I'm getting pretty tired of his temper tantrums and the way he pushes us around."

"Well, he won't push these celebrities around."

"Look at him, so impressed by these big-shot movie stars, trying to get them to like him."

"You certainly aren't trying," Kelly said.

"Why should I? They're just human beings who happen to have a glamorous job. They're no better than you or me. I hope you remember that; stay as down-to-earth as usual and don't let these movie stars fool you."

Kelly made a face. "Mickey Pines didn't even try to fool me—blowing smoke and yawning in my face. And I think he slept in his clothes. Ugh!"

"Not everyone shares your opinion." Alex nodded toward Cheri and Maxi, who were walking on either side of Mickey and laughing with him.

"They have no taste," Kelly exclaimed. "I don't know what I expected, but it wasn't this. As far as I'm concerned, Mickey Pines is a slob."

They all regrouped around the side of the mansion as Steve continued the tour.

"This is the formal English garden." Steve's arm swept over an expanse of yellow lawn. "Or rather, it *was* the garden." He grinned when everyone laughed.

"Steve is really laying on the charm," Kelly whispered. "I'd like to see him treating us that well." She laughed delightedly at the idea.

"Is this a private joke or can anyone join in?" Mickey Pines was standing directly behind her. She almost jumped out of her skin.

"Uh, I guess it's private." She lowered her eyes in confusion.

Mickey grinned and gave her an odd little salute. Then he joined the other celebrities.

"What's the matter with you?" Alex said. "You're bright red."

"Nothing, I was just startled. I didn't hear him coming."

"You're all flushed." He stared at her suspiciously. "Are you sure you're not, you know, attracted to Pines after all?"

"Of course not," she exclaimed. "I told you, Alex, he's disgusting. And certainly no big deal. He's just a boy—he looks about nineteen, *your* age—who happens to be a movie star. And an incredibly arrogant boy at that."

"Well, remember who your real friends are," Alex said, nudging her.

She brushed Alex's hand off her arm lightly.

"Look, everyone's going into the house. Good, I need to warm up."

Inside the front door was a lovely foyer with a marble floor, yellow-and-white rugs, and twenty-foot-high windows with deep blue velvet drapes. A circular stairway led upstairs.

"Better than any studio set," Franklyn Deeds cracked, rubbing his hands against his leather pants.

"I have to thank my assistant, Alex, here," Steve said, "for helping us get permission to shoot in Windward Point. The owners, the Northrop-Smiths, are friends of Alex's father. They don't often allow people like us in for photographs."

Kelly, standing next to the other models, didn't miss the whispered words that Maxi and Cheri exchanged.

"That Alex must be some catch," Maxi muttered. "He's gotta be loaded."

"Too young for me," Cheri complained, "loaded or not."

"You're kidding." Maxi snorted. "What's wrong with a younger man? Especially a rich one!"

"Nothing," Cheri said lazily. "But I'm twenty-three and Alex looks like a college kid. If you want to know who I'd go after, take a look behind you."

Kelly didn't have to turn around to know who they were talking about. Mickey Pines, of course. But Kelly was puzzled. She leaned forward to tap Maxi's shoulder.

"Uh, excuse me, Maxi—isn't Mickey Pines a teenager? He makes all those high-school movies."

Maxi and Cheri laughed together. "Sure, he plays eighteen-year-olds, but he's really twenty-four," Cheri said. "They always use older actors to play high-school kids. They don't trust the real thing. You know, I once read that Mickey put on twenty pounds for a role, to fill out his face so he'd look younger. But he looks terrific to me now! You go after Alex," she told Maxi. "I'll try my luck with Mr. Pines."

"That's fine with me," Maxi said. "The less competition, the better. So it's settled," she said, ignoring Kelly completely. "Alex is for me, Mickey is all yours."

As Kelly watched, incredulous, Cheri walked right up to Mickey.

"Hi again. Seems like we may be spending lots of time together." Lazily, she brushed blond bangs out of her eyes. "I don't suppose you have a match, do you?"

Mickey grinned knowingly, as if he was used to flimsy excuses to get his attention. "I just gave up smoking," he drawled.

"What a coincidence, so did I." Cheri laughed gaily and threaded her arm through Mickey's. "Smoking is so bad for you!"

She led him away from the group. Kelly found Alex. "Did you see that?" she asked. "What a disgusting show."

"What's really disgusting is that Mickey didn't mind."

Kelly tossed her head. "It's a good thing I'm not impressed by Mickey Pines. If that's the kind of girl he likes, I don't think much of his taste."

Steve led them into a large, paneled room.

"This is the formal dining room," he announced. "The kitchen and pantry are downstairs, but we won't go down there now."

"You'll see them later," Marilyn, the art director, added. "We have the most adorable setup in mind for that area—the French maid in the pantry kissing Sir Ernest, while Fiona sits in the dining room, totally oblivious."

"I hardly think that's suitable," Fiona Kendall protested.

"Which young lady do I get to kiss?" Sir Ernest gazed eagerly at Maxi, Cheri, and Kelly, and Kelly hastily turned her eyes away.

"You're not giving passionate kisses to anyone except me," Fiona declared in a shrill voice.

"My dear, I haven't kissed *you* passionately in thirty years."

"Come on, folks!" Steve was looking desperate. "We haven't even begun—let's keep our tempers in check." He took out a handkerchief and mopped his brow.

"All right, I'll solve everything," Marilyn announced. "We'll have Mickey play a *young* man who kisses the maid . . . Uh, Kelly, you'll do fine!"

"Me?" Kelly stammered.

"I think that works out well, don't you all?" Marilyn asked, pleased with her quick thinking. "Mickey will be perfect as the romantic guest."

Kelly heard someone laugh out loud behind her. She turned around and found herself eye to eye with Mickey Pines. He winked at her.

Kelly flushed a deep red and whirled around. "Uh, don't you think Cheri is more the French-maid type?" she said hastily.

"You know, she may be right," Steve said. "Cheri's got more curves than Kelly. She's blond and cuddly, while Kelly's more the athletic type. Cheri would be perfect."

"Okay—I like it," Marilyn declared. "Now let me describe the sitting-room scene." She led the way into the next room.

"Alex," Steve called, "take notes in here—we'll have to block off these windows and bounce light in from reflectors."

Kelly stayed behind in the dining room as the others moved on. She was already feeling fed up with the personalities involved in the shoot. *Two whole days of this!* she thought mournfully, pretending to examine the fancy woodwork on the wall.

She noticed an unusual box-shaped seam in one wall. *They sure put a lot of detail into these old houses*, she thought. She leaned closer to the wall to poke at a couple of buttons set into the paneling near the seam, wondering what on earth they could be for. *Maybe the wall will open up to reveal a secret room—these old houses are full of mysterious things like that!*

"Where's Kelly?" she heard Steve say in the next room, just as a creaking noise sounded behind the boxlike seam in the wall. *My gosh, what have I done?* Kelly thought frantically. She turned around and flattened herself against the wall behind her, trying to cover up the buttons. But the wall was no longer there! She felt herself falling backward into empty space. She sat down hard on a shelf that seemed to have replaced the wall. "Help!" she yelled.

She found herself looking out into the dining room from inside a musty-smelling hole, her legs poking out in front of her. As she twisted around, the shelf under her moved slightly. "Help me!" she screamed again.

Three

Mickey Pines suddenly appeared and sprang forward, reaching out to Kelly. Then he had hold of her and was pulling, his hands under her arms.

"Don't fight me," he commanded as she flailed at him. Kelly obeyed and let Mickey pull her out and set her on her feet.

"What on earth—" Kelly stared from Mickey to the hole in the wall.

"Hey, it's all right. . . . You're okay now." Mickey's voice was strong and soothing.

By this time everyone had rushed into the dining room.

Cheri's mouth dropped open. "It's a dumb-waiter! Did this ditzy kid fall in?"

Franklyn Deeds and Rebecca Halloway looked

annoyed, as if Kelly had set out to bother them personally.

Alex pushed past the others. "Kelly, are you okay? What happened?"

"I've never seen a dumbwaiter before. I guess I did fall in." Now that she was safe, Kelly felt deeply humiliated.

But Mickey put a finger under her chin, grinning at her. "Hello, Kelly. . . . Speak to us. Are you all right?"

Why, he is good looking, she thought, smiling back. "I'm okay . . . just embarrassed."

Alex glared at Mickey. "She's fine, so why don't you take your hands off her?"

"Okay, don't get sore." Mickey lifted his hands in the air, grinning impishly. "I'm unarmed."

Sir Ernest was studying the dumbwaiter with interest. "All these old houses had dumbwaiters to lift trays from the basement kitchen to the dining room." He showed them the control buttons. "Somehow, Kelly pushed the button that summoned this one. But, my dear, how did you get inside?"

Rebecca Halloway began to laugh, and soon everyone joined in.

Kelly forced a laugh herself. "Well, uh, I just pushed the button to see what it was. And then I leaned back—and I guess I leaned too far."

"A dumbwaiter." Steve shook his head in disgust. "It really isn't funny. Alex," he ordered impatiently, "move a chair or something in front of that thing. I don't want anyone else falling into it and hurting themselves. This is ridiculous."

Maxi snorted. "Some people will do anything for a little attention. Imagine pulling a stunt like that."

"I'll say," Cheri agreed. But the look she gave Kelly was full of envy.

Mickey grinned. "I've had girls fall for me, but no one ever went through a wall before." Chuckling, he gave Kelly an approving look that made her bristle.

"That's enough," Steve said. "Alex, see to this wall, then join the rest of us upstairs. We still have work to do today. Lisa, you take the ladies upstairs into wardrobe. I'll show the men where their dressing room is. Kelly, you're in the first setup with Mickey. Let's try to keep the pranks to a minimum, okay?"

Kelly's face flamed as she followed Lisa up the main stairs obediently.

"Good job," Cheri muttered at her. "I didn't know there was going to be a competition for Mickey Pines around here. I guess I misjudged your baby face."

"There isn't any competition."

"Right, you keep telling yourself that." Cheri swept up the stairs ahead of her.

"Save your breath," Amy, the young editor, advised. "She's already made up her mind about you."

"But I didn't plan to fall into the dumbwaiter so

Mickey could rescue me," Kelly told Amy. "Why would I do such a stupid thing?"

"Okay, okay, I believe you." Amy grinned. "It was only a lucky accident. But between you and me, if anyone is going to get Mickey Pines during this shoot, I'd rather it was you than Cheri or Maxi."

"What? I don't even like him," she protested. "I can't stand his type—he's conceited, self-centered, and arrogant."

"Nevertheless, I saw sparks between you two," Amy insisted. "Whether you know it or not, Kelly—you've been hit by Cupid's little arrow."

It did Kelly no good to protest. Amy only chuckled at her explanations.

"This is the ladies' dressing area," Lisa announced. "How do you like it? It's really the master bedroom suite."

"This is a bedroom?" Kelly had never seen such a bedroom. It was enormous—but she'd been prepared for that. What she hadn't been prepared for was the cozy private screening room at one end of the massive suite, fitted with cushiony sofas.

"Pretty wild, huh?" Amy eyed the extravagant quarters approvingly. "For those quiet evenings at home, when you feel like watching your favorite movies with a few dozen intimate friends."

Kelly was torn between awe and disdain. "It seems so—"

"Excessive," Amy finished for her. "It makes you wonder if some people just aren't *too* rich."

The rest of the suite consisted of a separate sitting room for Mr. and Mrs. Northrop-Smith, as well as a bathroom and a dressing area for each. Kelly stopped to examine one mirror-lined closet—it looked almost as big as her bedroom at home! The closets, to her disappointment, were empty.

"Their clothes must be in storage for the winter," Amy said. "Too bad, I'd love to see what kind of wardrobe Mrs. Northrop-Smith has."

"What a bother," Kelly said in her best British accent, "maintaining one's wardrobe can be *such* a bore." They laughed together.

Oliver, the makeup artist, was waiting in the powder room to do Kelly's face for the first setup.

He greeted her warmly, instantly putting her at her ease. It was always a little difficult to let a total stranger take over her looks, and Kelly appreciated Oliver's attention. He was careful to explain everything he did.

"I'm going to make you up like a flapper, but I'm not going to imitate real twenties makeup," he assured her as she turned her back to slip off her sweater and pull on a makeup robe. Kelly was still uncomfortable undressing before make-up artists and stylists, though most of the models she'd met didn't give it a second thought. "I'm going to modify the heavy pancake makeup they used back then, and the white face-powder— you'd look like a wax doll by today's standards."

Working quickly and skillfully, Oliver applied sheer makeup base and fixed a primer on Kelly's lips and eyelids. Next, he dusted a light coating of subtle pink powder over her entire face and neck and shoulders, let it settle, and then expertly whisked most of it away. The result was a soft, glowing skin that looked natural, yet flawless.

Oliver reached for the gel blusher, bent close to Kelly's face, and then straightened up without adding the color to her skin. "You don't need much blusher on those cheeks," he laughed. "Either you've got a gorgeous natural complexion or you're in love."

"Oh," Kelly stuttered, "it's—it must be the heat. It's so warm in here."

"I don't really need to heighten your color," Oliver said, "but just for fun, I'm going to make the color into a definite shape to look like the cartoon image of a flapper, with a circle of rouge on each cheek."

"Won't that look awfully silly?"

Oliver concentrated on drawing two perfect circles on Kelly's cheeks. "Not at all . . . See, it's fairly subtle, but humorous. Now we'll do the mouth."

"But I never draw such a harsh outline on my lips," Kelly protested in horror.

Oliver frowned. "If you insist on talking I'll never finish. There, now tell me you don't look spectacular. That sparkle in your eyes is priceless! I wish makeup could add that glow, but only one thing will do that—love." Oliver packed up his brushes.

"I'm afraid you're wrong this time," Kelly told him firmly. "I'm not in love with anyone. At least, not anyone here, that's for sure."

As Oliver cleaned up, Pepe, the hairdresser, came in and went quickly to work, tugging and pulling at Kelly's head until she thought she might scream.

"What are you doing?" she finally burst out. "It hurts! And I never wear my hair parted in the middle and pulled back like that—it looks so severe."

Pepe held a fringed and beaded headband across her forehead, squinting at the effect.

"Be patient—it will be fantastic," he assured her, but she was still doubtful.

"I know my own face," she fussed, furrowing her brow to keep the headband's fringe from tickling her eyebrows. "One thing my mother always told me, pulled-back hair doesn't flatter me."

Pepe ignored her nervous chatter, working efficiently while Kelly told him all the reasons why the hairstyle would be a disaster.

"Look," Pepe finally commanded. "Look at the whole effect."

Kelly's mouth dropped in astonishment as Pepe stood aside and she saw her reflection in the brightly lit mirror. She'd been transformed. Her thick curly hair had been pulled back into the tight bun she'd always despised, but the beaded band across her forehead, just above her eyes, offset the severity of the hairstyle. Pepe had crimped her hair into gentle waves over her temples, and as he handed her a mirror and swiveled her chair so she could inspect the back, she realized that the intricately knotted bun looked stunning.

"I love it!" she said. "I'm sorry, Pepe—you knew best."

"I get paid to know best," he said smugly. "Now go get dressed."

Lisa led her back into the dressing area. "Now strip and try this number on. It should fit perfectly—I had it altered to your measurements. I'd hate to stick pins into this fabulous silk."

"It's beautiful," Kelly said, taking the dress from Lisa. It had a deep diagonal ruffle from one shoulder down to the low-cut top. The glowing rose color would flatter her skin tones, and the fabric felt satiny smooth.

Kelly loosened her makeup robe. As instructed, she'd worn a sheer strapless bra and seamless panty hose that morning under her regular clothes—but now she paused uncertainly. Pepe was still in the powder room behind her.

"When will I ever get used to this business," she mumbled, trying to make a joke out of her modesty. "I hate to dress and undress in front of men all the time—and I hate myself for caring about it. Most models don't."

Lisa smiled in amusement. "You'll get used to it," she assured her.

The dress slid over Kelly's head and Lisa tugged it into place. "Actually, Kelly, it's nice to work with someone as *real* as you for a change. You're so sweet."

"Sweet! Why doesn't anyone ever think I'm sophisticated?" She smiled at Lisa.

"Of course you are," Lisa said, straightening the seams of the filmy dress. "There, that should feel comfortable now."

Kelly stepped toward the full-length mirror for her first look.

"Wow," she exclaimed. She looked fantastic! The flirty dress stopped just above the knee, and there wasn't much fabric between the short hem and the low-cut top.

"You look plenty sophisticated in that," Lisa said.

"Do I look . . . at least twenty?" Kelly asked hopefully.

"Honey, in that dress you're ageless. Definitely old *enough*."

Kelly beamed.

"But those stockings are the worst." Lisa plowed through her huge accessory bag, tossing panty hose all over the bed. "Try these glittery ones; something with pizzazz, to pull the look together with the shoes."

"Will the shoes show?"

"They're featured accessories, and at four hundred bucks a pair, you'd better believe we'll make them show!"

The shoes were satin, the same rose color as

the dress, with a stripe of black snakeskin across the vamp that fastened with a rhinestone clip. They were the most elaborate shoes Kelly had ever worn.

"This is fun, isn't it?" Suddenly, Kelly was totally lighthearted. "It's like dressing for a part in a movie. This must be what movie stars feel like."

She didn't even mind that she had to pull three pairs of panty hose off and on, unclasping and removing the shoes each time, before Lisa was satisfied with her look.

Then Lisa hung a small black beaded purse over Kelly's arm at the elbow, warning her to hold her wrist up to keep the bag from sliding off her arm.

"I know, it's a featured accessory," Kelly said.

"Wait, we need earrings, and what about a necklace?"

After a short fuss, they finally fastened long drop earrings to Kelly's ear lobes. They were made of rhinestones, like the shoe buckles.

Lisa held up several necklaces. "No, these aren't right. Flappers wore long, long strands of beads, down to their knees, but that would be all wrong with that diagonal neckline. I know, Kelly, toss these beads over one shoulder!"

"You mean, like this?" Kelly slipped a strand of pearl beads and a couple of shiny jeweled ropes over her head and across her chest, following the direction of the ruffle.

"I like it. It works," Lisa declared happily. "It's completely divine!"

She ushered Kelly out of the bedroom and up the curved stairway to the floor above. Amy was waiting for them there, and she nodded in appreciation at Kelly's outfit.

"Will you explain the layout for me?" Kelly asked.

"Well, this is a period piece, a twenties theme," Amy answered. "A bootlegger and his gun moll are pouring the ingredients for bathtub gin into the sunken marble tub."

"Gin—in a bathtub?" Kelly asked.

"During prohibition, when drinking alcohol was illegal, people used to brew their own beer and wine and gin, supposedly in bathtubs. It's a fun idea for a shot, so enjoy yourself. Marilyn wants this spread to be lighthearted; a romp through fall fashions!"

"Fall fashions," Kelly muttered. "I'll never get used to the lead time on these magazine shoots. Here it is, nearly winter, but we've already finished winter, spring, and summer layouts. It gets confusing."

"That's the least of my confusion," Amy said. "Here we are, the guest bathroom."

Four

The room looked more like a study than a bathroom, as far as Kelly was concerned. It was practically as big as the living room in her own house. In the wide entryway there were cushioned chairs and bookshelves and stacks of magazines. The back of the room contained a sink, a separate stall shower and the sunken marble tub Amy had mentioned. But these were far more elegant than any ordinary bathroom fixtures.

"All the trim is brass," Marilyn told them, "taken from a luxury cruise ship."

Kelly marveled at the stained glass in the windows and the elaborate crystal chandelier that threw patterns of sparkling light onto the pink marble floor.

"Now I'll just check Mickey one more time, make sure he's dashing and dapper."

"Him?" Kelly sniffed in disdain. "I don't see how you'll make him look dashing and dapper. He's more the kind who would sit around in his undershirt with a beer can."

Amy stifled a laugh. "I hope not. Kelly, why don't you open your eyes and take another look?"

Kelly laughed. "I don't need another look. You'll never convince me otherwise." She glanced contemptuously at Mickey, standing on the other side of the bathroom. His back was to her, but he would manage to look crude even in the fancy white suit, she was sure of that.

Amy shook her head. "Mickey," she called, "let's take another look at you."

"Can't a guy get any peace?" he joked. "I already feel ridiculous in this getup." He angled his white felt hat over one eye and straightened his tie as he turned around and walked toward Amy. Kelly's eyes opened wide.

"Kelly Blake—get a look at you." He whistled in admiration, then gently lifted Kelly's hand, holding it high and turning her so he could see every angle.

"You're not bad yourself," she said. Mickey was unbelievably handsome. He had bathed and shaved, and now, dressed in the close-fitting white wool suit, he was not only wide-awake and cheerful, but as dashing and dapper as Amy might wish.

He sported a white vest that matched the suit

and a shocking-pink silk dress-shirt with a lighter pink tie. A heavy gold watch fob was draped across the vest front, and he wore a gold tie bar that matched his heavy gold cuff links. He carried a black ebony cane and wore white spats over his black patent leather shoes. With his eyes shaded by the hat, he looked dangerous, daring—and totally irresistible.

"I feel really silly," he said. Kelly felt a surge of sympathy for him.

"You look great." She grinned. If Mickey could confess to feeling silly, she couldn't remain angry about the episode with the dumbwaiter. Maybe he wasn't so arrogant after all.

He looked at her, abashed. "Are you sure? Who ever heard of a guy wearing a bright pink shirt like this?"

Kelly shook her head emphatically. "That shirt is fantastic," she assured him. "Perfect for the suit. It's an original, isn't it, Lisa?"

"This girl knows her fashions," Lisa said. "That shirt is only worth about three hundred big ones."

Mickey whistled again. "Too rich for my blood."

Steve interrupted their conversation. "Kelly and Mickey, stand over by that spotlight. I need to take some meter readings."

"This is the most boring part," Kelly told Mickey as they took their places. "Setting the lights. Once that's done, it takes no time to get the shots."

Mickey nodded, grateful for the information. "Hey, listen," he said, "I hope I wasn't too rough on you before."

"Rough?" She acted baffled. "I don't know what you mean."

"Giving you a hard time about the dumbwaiter. I thought it was a typical female trick, like Cheri might pull." He examined her face thoughtfully. "But you're not like her, are you?"

Kelly was flustered by his intense gaze. "No . . . uh, I'm not like that," she stuttered. "And you weren't rough at all. In fact, I should thank you for rescuing me."

"My pleasure." For once, Mickey's mocking look was completely gone. "I guess it could have happened to anyone. In fact, if I'd known that dumbwaiter was there, I would have tried to pack Steve Hollender into it first thing."

Kelly laughed. "Oh, Steve's a pain, but he's a terrific photographer. He just gets a little grumpy at times."

"Grumpy isn't the word," Mickey said. "He was really annoyed with you for having an accident. I mean, he seemed to think you'd done it on purpose."

"Steve is a little suspicious of people at times," Kelly agreed.

"Hmmm. My guess is, Steve's the type who likes all the models to fall in love with him, and you're one model that didn't."

Kelly stared in surprise. Mickey was right. Steve had taken her out to a fancy party the first week she'd met him, trying to impress her. The date had been a disaster. If it hadn't been for Meg Dorian, Steve would have completely abandoned Kelly when she insisted she had to get home by midnight.

"You don't know how right you are," Kelly said. "How did you guess?"

"I'm kind of an expert on the ways guys use girls," Mickey said.

"I suppose you know all the tricks."

"Don't judge me before you know me."

Kelly felt immediately contrite. "I'm sorry, I shouldn't have said that. But you do seem awfully sure of yourself."

Mickey shrugged. "Why not? That's part of being an actor. I'm always sure of myself when I'm acting. Even so, acting is a gamble, and I'm not a gambler by nature. I like to know exactly what I'm doing. I've been lucky in this business, and I found out I'm pretty sharp. I've planned it all carefully."

"Well, I sort of fell into modeling. Meg Dorian—she's the head of the FLASH! modeling agency—spotted me at a makeover session that *Miss* magazine did in a shopping mall near where I live."

"I guess you fall into a lot of things," Mickey cracked, and Kelly burst out laughing.

"Sometimes I do," she agreed. Mickey's eyes lit up when he really laughed, she noticed. He had a nice face. She no longer found his cocky attitude annoying. In fact, he seemed exactly like the kind

of guy he played in the movies—the tough boy
with the soft heart. It was a very appealing
combination.

"That guy Alex, Steve's assistant," Mickey
said. "He seems to be a special friend of yours."

"Yes, I know Alex. We go out sometimes,"
Kelly admitted. "But I don't date anyone exclusively."

A little-boy grin spread across Mickey's face.
"That's just the kind of news I wanted to hear."

Kelly smiled casually, but inside, she was
breathless. She couldn't believe it—Mickey
Pines, the actor, was laughing and talking with
her, ignoring everyone else. Mickey Pines, a
genuine movie star, was interested in her! What a
shoot this was going to be.

"Okay, you two," Steve barked, "the lights are
set, so let's get ready for the test shots."

"You look great," Amy called. "Kelly, you're a
perfect flapper, and Mickey, you could sell me
bathtub gin any day."

"I still feel strange in this getup."

"Oh, you're wrong," Kelly told him, "you were
made for those clothes." Dimly, she was aware of
Alex watching her as he made the final lighting
adjustments in the room. *Oh, well*, she thought,
*it isn't as though I was just flattering Mickey. He
does look smashing*.

And she knew she looked good, too, from the
way Mickey's eyes followed her when Steve
began posing her. She couldn't help glancing at

Mickey from the corner of her eye. She found it hard to concentrate on what Steve was saying.

Relax, she kept telling herself; *he's just an ordinary human being like you, or Alex, or anyone.* But her pulse was racing with excitement.

Movie stars aren't ordinary, no matter what Alex says! Millions of people, millions, recognize Mickey when he walks down the street. Thousands and thousands read about his private life and buy magazines and newspapers so they can find out who his latest flame is.

What would it be like to go out with him? Mystery Woman Latest Flame in Mickey Pines's Heart . . . Kelly Blake was reached for comment in her swank Manhattan apartment yesterday . . . "Mickey and I are very special friends," said Miss Blake, the hottest new model out of the FLASH! Agency . . . Will wedding bells ring?

"Hey—Kelly, where'd you go?" Mickey, posing next to her, snapped his fingers in front of her face.

"Wake up, Kelly!" Steve snapped a couple of polaroid shots to test the lighting and the poses. "Okay, relax while these develop."

"Sorry . . . I do that sometimes," Kelly told Mickey, forcing a laugh. "I guess I'm a real dreamer. I was thinking that you looked different in real life than you do in your movies."

Mickey seemed insulted. "Don't pull any of that movie star stuff with me, all right? I'm just a regular person, like anybody else."

"Maybe. I mean, I know that's how *you* must feel inside—but I still have to get used to the fact that I'm standing here, talking to a movie star."

"You're really something, you know that?" Mickey eyed her in delight. "The ladies I've been meeting lately would never say anything like that." He laughed ruefully. "Either they pretend they can't remember who I am, or else they try to get a part in one of my movies."

"I wouldn't do that. For one thing, I'm not actress material. Believe me, I know. I messed up my first TV commercial not too long ago. I don't think I'll ever act again."

"Maybe you had the wrong director." Mickey grasped her chin, turning her head to get a better look at her profile. "Show me anger, show me fear," he commanded.

Kelly burst out laughing. "It's hopeless," she cried.

Mickey threw an arm over her shoulder. "Hey, there are too many actresses in the world, anyway."

Alex bumped into them. "Sorry," he muttered. "Just trying to get this reflector in the right place." He glared at Kelly.

Mickey looked at Alex and back at Kelly. "Guess I'll go have a cigarette until Steve is ready."

Kelly tapped Alex's arm. "So, stranger, how's it going? Think I make a good flapper?"

"You make a good flirt," he grumbled. "I guess hanging around movie stars agrees with you."

"Don't be silly, Alex, I wasn't flirting. And, anyway, Mickey doesn't act like a movie star. He's a regular person, just like you said. He's very considerate and levelheaded. He didn't make me feel at all embarrassed about falling into the dumbwaiter."

"That must've been hard, because it was a pretty embarrassing thing to do."

Her temper flared. "Mickey didn't think so; he didn't insult me about it. Actually, I was lucky he was there to save me—because you weren't there when I needed you. Mickey was fantastic, admit it."

"Yeah, a daring rescue—just like in the movies," Alex said bitterly.

"I think you're jealous! Come on," she needled him, trying to tickle him under his chin, "admit it. Alex is jealous!"

"Cut it out! I'm working, and you're being ridiculous." Rudely, Alex brushed her hand away.

"I don't know why you're acting so nasty about it. Mickey's nice and I like him. Besides, I noticed Maxi coming on to you before, and you didn't exactly give her the cold shoulder. There's a real gold digger if I ever saw one. You should've seen her eyes light up when Steve mentioned your rich father."

Alex scowled. "So that's the only reason any girl would like me, is it, because my father's rich? I don't suppose Maxi could be attracted to me, the way you're attracted to Mickey Pines?"

"I'm not attracted to him. I'm just interested in meeting new people."

"Good, because he'd never be interested in you."

"As a matter of fact, he is interested. He thinks I'm . . . different."

Alex laughed out loud. "You're different all right."

"You don't have to insult me. Come on, Alex, at least Mickey seems to like me for myself. He's not after anything, like Maxi is with your money."

"Maybe I should be thankful girls like Maxi find me attractive."

"I have no idea what type of man Maxi is interested in," Kelly said huffily. "And I hardly care. You're just saying all this because you're jealous, but I told you, I only find Mickey interesting."

"And Maxi finds *me* interesting," Alex snapped.

"Good, then this job seems promising for both of us!"

"You're right, it does. So maybe we'd better cancel our plans for tonight," he said coldly. "You'll probably be with Mr. Wonderful instead."

"Fine," she snapped angrily. "Oh, but how am I going to get home?"

Alex stared at her coolly. "Hasn't your darling Mickey offered to drive you to New Jersey yet? Or is that too much effort for an important movie star?"

"Alex," she said, trying to control her temper,

"I barely talked to the guy. He hasn't asked me for a date."

"I'm surprised—you're such a smooth operator."

Kelly's cheeks flamed with anger. "I'm not *operating* at all—I simply met a nice person that I'll be working with for a while, and I tried to be friendly with him. I can't be a successful professional without knowing how to relate to all kinds of people, you know."

"Spare me the lecture." Alex turned away. "Some of us have work to do."

"You really make me furious! You're making a big deal out of nothing, Alex, and you don't understand me at all!"

"So what? Mickey does."

"Look, Alex, I never complain about a job, but modeling is hard work, and it helps to have a friend around. I was really counting on you as a friend."

"You don't know what friends are for, apparently."

"Fine, then let's just forget it. Forget about driving me home, and forget about driving me to the mansion tomorrow too. I'll make my own arrangements, if that's how you want it."

"No, Kelly, that's how *you* want it." He turned his back on her.

Steve beckoned to Alex. "I'm not happy with the light quality in here. Let's try something else, maybe some natural light and filters. Get Lisa to help you move those reflectors, Alex. We're losing time."

Determined, Kelly marched up to the art director. "Marilyn, I have a small problem. Could I get a car service to take me back and forth to New Jersey for the rest of the shoot?"

Marilyn glanced at her watch. "Talk to Arlene about that," she said irritably. "We'll take it out of Steve's expenses when he bills the magazine."

"What's this about car troubles?" Mickey appeared at Kelly's side, as if he knew she had another problem.

"It's nothing, really," she explained. "I, uh, was just thinking how annoying it is to have to depend on getting rides from friends. I'll have to use a hired car from now on."

"Why don't you drive your own car?"

"Well, uh, naturally, I'd prefer to use my own car," she said quickly, hoping he wouldn't find out she wasn't old enough to drive, "but I'm barely awake in the morning, and we have to leave so early—I couldn't deal with all that traffic!"

"Commuting's no fun," he agreed. "I'm not a morning person, either." Then his face lit up with that delighted little-boy look. "I know, why don't we share a limo? We could ride back and forth together to the city."

"Oh, that would be . . ." Wait a minute, what was she thinking? She couldn't ride with Mickey; she'd have to go into Manhattan. And she might have a problem leaving right after the day's work was over if she did ride with Mickey. But she couldn't tell him the truth—that she had to go right home to do her homework. Her parents had been adamant about that.

"Well, it's lovely of you to offer, but," she took a deep breath, "actually, I live in New Jersey."

"So? The chauffeur doesn't care where you live, and neither do I."

"Oh. Well. That's nice of you, but . . . I have some previous family commitments this week, and it wouldn't be fair to make you change your schedule to fit mine . . ."

Mickey raised his eyebrows. "Listen, if you're involved with someone, just say so."

"Believe me," she said, feeling a knot of disappointment in her stomach, "if I could think of a way to drive with you, I would."

"Family commitments, huh?"

"Mickey, it's true, I do have to do something for my mother and father these two nights. Well, actually, he's my stepfather—my mother remarried."

She couldn't believe what she heard herself saying—she almost never even thought of Hal Blake as her stepfather, let alone mentioned it. Jennifer knew, but to the rest of the world, Hal Blake was her father—and he was, in every way that counted. And the point was, she couldn't let her parents down no matter how much she wanted to be with Mickey.

Mickey shrugged. "It's too bad about the ride. But if you really get stuck, let me know."

"I will."

She breathed a sigh of relief. That had been a close call and she'd nearly blown it. *Not that it's a disgrace to live with your family—most sixteen-year-olds do. But Mickey simply can't find out my real age, that I have homework to do at night. It'll ruin everything.*

Guiltily, she checked to make sure Alex hadn't overheard her conversation with Mickey. He hadn't—he was still busy rearranging the lights. *Now if only Alex doesn't tell Mickey. I'll just have to keep them as far apart as possible. Right now, that ought to be easy!*

Five

When the lights were ready Steve took several shots. First he photographed Kelly holding a champagne glass, kicking one foot up behind her as Mickey poured a splash of gin (it was really plain club soda) into her glass. Then Mickey put his arm around Kelly's waist as Kelly bent backward. He really had to hold her tight to balance the pose. Lisa stuck a cigarette holder between Mickey's lips.

"Now look relaxed," Steve commanded, staring intently into the camera.

"Relaxed?" Mickey said incredulously. The cigarette holder fell from his lips and clattered onto the floor, and everyone laughed. Giggling, Kelly let her head rest against Mickey's vest.

"Uh-oh—makeup," Lisa cried. "You've soiled his vest—I'll have to rub that off before it stains!"

"Oh, I'm sorry," Kelly exclaimed, chagrined—but Mickey just winked at her.

"I shoulda wore black," he said, slurring his words as if he were drunk from the gin. Everyone laughed again, and Kelly felt grateful toward Mickey. He was really helping to keep things light, easing the strain so that no tempers were lost, which often happened during a tense shot.

The makeup came off Mickey's vest, and Oliver retouched Kelly's face. When Steve began posing her again, Kelly realized she was having the time of her life. She'd never felt more relaxed or more responsive to the camera, and she knew these shots were going to be among the best she'd done yet.

There was a feeling of excitement and recklessness in the air, and their poses got more and more seductive. Kelly felt every inch the slinky flapper, and if she hadn't known the "gin" was only club soda, she would've sworn she was giddily drunk.

"I think you're having an effect on me," she told Mickey as they posed for their final shot.

"You ain't seen nothing yet." He had his arms around her waist, and their heads were close together as they balanced precariously on the edge of the bathtub. Suddenly, he bent her back even further and gave her a kiss right out of an old-time movie.

"Perfect," Steve called. "Just perfect!"

Kelly came up for air, feeling not only breathless but dizzy. She could see Mickey's eyes shining wickedly.

"You took advantage of me," she scolded.

"I apologize," he said—but he didn't look the least bit sorry.

"Apologize, nothing!" Steve was totally thrilled. "That was great. Good instincts, Mickey. You two have real chemistry—these are going to be stupendous!"

Even the art director, who wasn't the type to give compliments, seemed impressed. "You looked pretty good," Marilyn said. "I think the folks at *Couture* will be pleased."

"Pleased!" Amy cried. "They're going to go nuts when they see these shots. Marilyn, you'll be the highest-paid art director in the business when this spread comes out!"

"We'll see," was all Marilyn would say. But everyone else was as excited as Amy and Steve.

"I can't wait to see the rest of the shots," Arlene cried. "This is turning into the best shoot I've been on all year."

"It's the talent," Steve said. "We're working with star quality here. Let's just take a couple more for good measure."

Mickey resumed his pose. "Your teeth are like stars . . ." he crooned at Kelly, "they come out at night."

"Oh, very funny. Not too original, though."

They grinned at each other as Steve continued shooting. In the back of her mind, Kelly was aware of Alex glowering at her from somewhere behind the camera, but all she could think of was Mickey, the way he'd kissed her, the way he made her laugh, the way his eyes never left her face.

Steve looked up from his camera and announced, "Okay, everyone, final shot of the morning."

"But seriously, folks . . ." Mickey began. Kelly waited for the joke.

"Doesn't she have the prettiest eyes you've ever seen?"

Her breath caught in her throat. Those blue eyes were so piercing, so intense.

"Kelly, you make me wish I'd been around in the Roaring Twenties—with you."

"That's a wrap," Steve called.

Mickey released her, and Lisa hurried to inspect the delicate white suit.

Kelly's head was spinning from Mickey's compliments. But had he really meant what he'd said, or was he just flattering her for the sake of a good shot? *He must've meant it*, she decided. He didn't seem the type to flatter anyone for the sake of a job. He hadn't flattered Maxi or Cheri, and he had to work with them, too.

"Let's break for lunch, people," Steve said. "Alex—strike this set, and let's get a head start on the next setup."

"What about lunch for Alex?" Maxi protested.

"I'll grab a sandwich when the set is down," Alex told her. "Besides, I'm not very hungry. The phoniness around here is enough to turn anyone's stomach."

He looked right at Kelly, but before she could say a word, Lisa had grabbed her arm and dragged her upstairs to remove the dress and her makeup.

Kelly eased the delicate silk over her hips. "I hate to take this off," she admitted.

"Don't worry, the others are just as gorgeous."

"It's a good thing I'm a fairly sensible person. This kind of thing could really turn your head."

Lisa gave her an amused look. "You're already turning heads, all right."

Kelly colored. Did Lisa, too, think Mickey liked her? Was it true? It was really too much to hope for, yet it seemed to be true. If only Jennifer or Paisley were there—she longed for a close friend that she could confide in and ask the questions swimming in her head.

"Better get your jeans back on," Lisa advised. "It'll be a while before the next setup is ready, and you'll only ruin your makeup if you eat lunch with it on."

Quickly, Kelly slipped into her own things, but left on a bit more makeup than she normally wore. She didn't want to look like some fresh-faced, clean-scrubbed high-school girl.

Just then Alex wandered into the dressing area. "Sorry," he mumbled. "I was looking for the men's dressing room."

"It's through those mirrored doors."

Alex hesitated. "Look, Kelly, I'm not really

lost. Let's talk—I hate fighting with you. Maybe I did overreact down there. It was tough, watching Pines make out with you like that, but I know it was all an act. Let's be friends again, okay? It'll make this job a lot easier." He raised his arm for a friendly handshake.

Kelly hesitated. "Do you really mean *friends*?" she asked, reluctant to let Alex think she was offering him something more.

Alex's hand wavered and fell. "Forget it," he said sharply. "Let's just leave things the way they are. I guess by now I should be used to the way you double up on boyfriends."

Kelly bristled. "That isn't fair, Alex. You never said I had to choose between you and Eric Powers."

"No, I didn't care about your high-school heart-throb. I know you'll get him out of your system eventually. But I'm not used to competing with movie stars."

"We don't have any agreements. You're free to date anyone you want—so don't tell me what to do."

"I'm just looking out for you, Kelly. Sometimes you're pretty naive, and you don't know what Mickey Pines is really like. Don't be fooled by that innocent little-boy act he's pulling. Remember the story about the Big Bad Wolf?"

"Oh, that's absurd. Where do you get your information, anyway? Fan magazines? How do you know anything about Mickey Pines?"

Alex shook his head sadly. "It's pathetic. You're

trying to act so cool about the whole thing, but anyone looking at you could read your mind. I've always said you're no good at hiding your feelings. They're written all over you. You're totally starstruck."

"That's insulting," she cried angrily, aware that the color was flooding into her cheeks, "and untrue! And I'm not as innocent as you think. Go on, get out of here and let me alone. I don't have time to listen to you, Alex, even if you had something worthwhile to say."

Alex slammed the door behind him. Kelly was sorry to see him so angry, but she couldn't help her feelings. She just didn't think of Alex the way he seemed to think of her. And she felt she had every right to see what, if anything, might develop between her and Mickey. She didn't have an exclusive relationship with any boy!

But of course, Mickey wasn't a boy—that was the whole point.

Lunch had been set up inside the glass-enclosed sun porch, and everyone was busy piling plates high with cold meats and salads and fruits. Steve was speaking earnestly to Mickey. Kelly paused near the door to help herself to a steaming cup of coffee, unsure if she should take a chair near Mickey or wait for someone else to ask her to sit down. These things were so complicated. She didn't want to be obvious and run to Mickey's side like a lovesick puppy, but if she acted indifferent he might ignore her. She never knew what to do!

With a thrill of excitement, she realized Mickey had seen her and was excusing himself from Steve, heading straight for her.

"That coffee looks good," he said easily. He had changed back into his crumpled jeans and sweater, but he didn't look sloppy anymore. He looked comfortable, and just as adorable as ever. Her hand shook slightly as she lifted her cup.

Mickey helped himself to coffee. "Whew, boiling hot. I know, why don't we take these outside and let them cool off."

"Outside?"

"Why not? There's plenty of sun. Why don't we take a walk on the beach, explore the grounds a little. We've got time."

"That's a wonderful idea!" Kelly smiled in delight. "I love the ocean, don't you? It's even better in fall or winter, when the beaches are deserted and you can walk for miles, enjoying the salty air. Walking on the beach is one of my favorite things."

"Mine, too," Mickey agreed easily. "But let's grab our coats first. No sense freezing to death outside."

"Okay. Um, should we tell anyone where we're going in case they need us?"

"I think they'll figure it out," Mickey said dryly. "There aren't many places to go around here."

"No, there aren't. My coat's in the hall. I'll run and get it."

Forgetting how hungry she'd been a moment before, Kelly hurriedly wrapped herself in her oversized parka, winding her muffler tightly around her neck.

"All set," she announced brightly as Mickey met her in the hall.

He eyed her approvingly. "And now for a little adventure."

"You know, there's nothing I like better than exploring a new place." Kelly lifted her head to take in deep gulps of the fresh air blowing off the ocean.

"Me, too," Mickey agreed. "That's one of the reasons I like to take time off between pictures. I need to get away, enjoy new places for a while, be by myself." He made a face. "And here I am, stuck in fancy clothes and *makeup*, of all things. Why do I do this to myself? Or why did my agent do it to me, I should say. This is as bad as doing a movie."

Kelly frowned. "But don't you enjoy doing movies? The excitement, the thrill . . ."

"Thrill?" Mickey smiled good-naturedly. "It's a job, like any other job, believe me."

"I can't believe that. Acting must be one of the most rewarding things there is. I wish I had undiscovered acting talent, but I know it isn't true."

"Modeling seems to be a lot like acting. You have to take direction, pretend to be someone you're not . . ." He tossed a smooth stone into the surf and watched it disappear.

"You don't sound very . . . pleased about your acting. Don't you like it?"

"Probably as much as you like modeling," he said sarcastically.

"But I *love* modeling," Kelly said, genuinely puzzled. "I love feeling like someone else, someone completely different from who I really am."

"Oh? And who are you really? Isn't this the genuine Kelly Blake?"

She smiled. "I don't mean I have a split personality, or anything, but model Kelly is, oh, glamorous, mysterious—very sophisticated sometimes and terribly adventuresome, not like the real me at all. Basically, I'm a pretty straightforward person." She shrugged humorously. "No hidden depths or anything."

"Oh yeah? Well, I like people with no hidden depths." Mickey stepped closer—close enough to sweep back the hair that was blowing wildly across her face and hold it in place. "I like knowing this is the real Kelly Blake. It is, isn't it?"

"Guaranteed," she said lightly. Mickey gazed into her eyes for a long moment, then suddenly dropped his hands, letting her hair blow free again. She realized she had been holding her breath. As he walked aimlessly ahead of her, she exhaled deeply.

"Everyone thinks acting is so glamorous," he said as she caught up to him. "Well, it isn't. It's boring and tiring and hard. At least, making movies is. What I'd really like is to do more stage work. That's where I started when I decided to be an actor."

"Is stage work that different?"

"Sure. In a play you build a character, sustain a mood, let the character grow with no interruptions. And the audience responds immediately, so you know if you're reaching them or not. Movies . . ." He laughed scornfully. "You do one scene fourteen times, everything out of order, no mood, no context . . ."

"Mickey, you must like something about your work."

"I always think I do, every time my agent finds a 'great' part for me. I read the script, psych myself up to play some fascinating character. My energy is going, I'm on the set, and then—boom! A big crashing disappointment. The sound is bad, the lighting is off. By the time we get around to shooting the scene, I'm bored out of my skull. But I do it, again and again."

"It must be hard," Kelly said sympathetically, "but still, you're so good at what you do. When you see the finished movie up there on a big screen, aren't you pleased?"

"Yeah, thrilled," he said cynically.

"Oh, come on, admit it. It must be terrific. Aren't you the least bit proud of yourself?"

"If you say so."

"I do. Come on, smile!" She teased him as if he were just another high-school kid, one of her friends. She had no idea where she got the nerve to act like that with a movie star, but Mickey affected her that way. On the one hand, she was totally in awe of who he was and the things he'd done. But on the other hand, he seemed like a sad puppy who just needed to be loved and pampered a little.

"Come on," she coaxed, "just one little smile?"

"I'll make *you* smile." He scooped her into his arms, running toward the waves breaking onto shore. She shrieked, terrified and happy. Just at the edge of the surf, he came to an abrupt halt.

"No more Hollywood talk—is it a deal?" He cocked one eyebrow at her, holding her out over the water.

She shrieked again as a wave crashed at their feet. "It's a deal!"

Mickey set her on her feet, and they shook hands firmly.

"But—I'll race you to the jetty!" She took off, running up the beach toward the long row of boulders that formed a breakwater nearby.

Kelly reached the jetty first. "Hurry up," she yelled. The rocks were slippery in places, but Kelly was confident and surefooted as she made her way to the end of the jetty. The sun was at its strongest at this time of day. By the time Mickey reached her, panting, she was basking in its warmth, lulled by the sound of the breaking waves.

"Hey, are you falling asleep?" Mickey started to sit beside her. "Watch it," he suddenly yelled, yanking her up by one arm. She glanced up and saw a giant wave coming.

"Whoa," she cried, laughing. Together, they stepped back, caught by a spray of splashing water. "That was close," she said. She whirled around to face Mickey, throwing him off balance by her move.

"Mickey!"

He slipped sideways and tried to throw himself onto the jetty, but his foot had wedged into a crevice. He fell awkwardly onto the boulders, his foot still trapped.

Kelly's breath caught in her throat. She forced herself to be calm. "Mickey, you're hurt!"

Six

Kelly peered between the boulders. "Your leg is really bleeding a lot."

Mickey clenched his teeth. "I'll be okay."

But he couldn't get up, and she could see how painful it was for him to move the trapped leg.

"Wait, I'll try to move this rock." Kneeling, she grasped one of the smaller stones that were lodged between the boulders, pinning his foot. She wiggled it back and forth. "Is that better?"

"Worse," he gasped. "Go for help."

One look at Mickey's pale face convinced her to stay. "No, I think I can get it." Grimacing with determination, she dug her fingers around the rock and pulled. It loosened and finally gave. Carefully, mindful of his wound, she lifted it clear. "Try to move now."

He grabbed her arm and steadied himself against her. Then he pulled the injured leg from between the two boulders.

"How bad is it?" Now that the leg was free, Kelly suddenly felt nauseated.

He pulled the torn leg of his pants above his ankle. "Just a scrape," he managed to say between deep breaths, but Kelly knew from the blood that it was worse than that.

"You'll have to lean on me," she said. "We'll go slowly."

Waves crashed over the rocks, splashing the wound with stinging salt water, and Mickey let out a cry of pain.

Kelly, trying not to think about how serious the injury could turn out to be, knew she had to do something. Mickey might lose a lot of blood before they made it back to the shore. She stopped and began to unwrap her scarf from around her neck.

"What are you doing?" Mickey stared, dumbfounded.

"Don't talk," she said sternly, lifting the scarf over her head. "Stand still."

"I'm not going anywhere, believe me."

While Mickey leaned most of his weight on her, Kelly wrapped the muffler tightly above the jagged cut on his leg.

"Ouch! Do you know what you're doing?"

"I wasn't a Girl Scout for nothing," she said. "Okay, now lean on me. Try not to put any weight on that leg. It's a good thing I'm tall," she added, trying not to let him see how worried she was.

"This is stupid. It's no big deal."

"Shh, don't talk, I mean it. That leg ought to be stitched," she said sharply. "It's a jagged cut, but at least it's clean. There doesn't seem to be any sand or gravel in it."

"What are you, Junior Doctor Kelly or something?"

"Listen, no jokes, okay? Save your strength; it's a long walk back to the house."

"It's a long hobble, you mean."

Slowly, and painfully for Mickey, they picked their way back up the jetty. Kelly wished they'd never come outside. It was all her fault, daring him out on the rocks like that when it was obvious he wasn't used to it. She was such a show-off . . .

It seemed to take hours before they reached the end of the rocks and stumbled down onto the beach. Walking there was no picnic, either. With every step, they sank into moist sand, making slow progress.

"It didn't seem . . . this far, the first time," Mickey said through gritted teeth.

"We're almost there." But it looked an impossibly long way to the mansion. They finally neared the house, and Kelly spotted people in the enclosed sun porch, lingering over coffee. Could they still be at lunch? An eternity seemed to have gone by.

"Hello . . . anyone! Steve!" Kelly hollered

and waved. "They see us," she said gratefully. "They're coming."

The last few yards had been a real struggle. Even though she knew Mickey was in no mortal danger, she was very much relieved to see Steve, Alex, and Lisa running to help.

"I've certainly enjoyed our little stroll." Mickey grinned wanly.

"What happened?" Steve demanded, helping Kelly to support Mickey.

Kelly quickly explained about the accident. "We have to get him to a hospital. Even though the bleeding seems to have stopped, it's a deep wound."

"This is all I need," Steve grumbled as he helped Mickey to the driveway. "Insurance, law suits, personal injury claims. Mickey, don't call your lawyer right away," he pleaded. "We can work something out."

"I'm sure no one will sue you," Kelly said irritably. "Honestly, Steve, can't you think of anyone but yourself at a time like this?"

Kelly and Steve guided Mickey onto the backseat of Steve's car. Alex, she noticed, hung back—as if Mickey had hurt himself on purpose to get Kelly's attention!

Amy ran outside. "I called the local hospital," she said breathlessly, "and told the hospital emergency room you were coming. Here are the directions."

"Check our liability insurance," Steve ordered.

"Where am I?" Mickey joked weakly as Kelly fastened the seat belt around him.

"Keep still," Kelly told him. "We're taking you to the hospital."

"How romantic."

Kelly started to close the car door, but Mickey grabbed her arm.

"You're coming with me," he ordered. "I'm not facing some local quack without my personal medical advisor, Doctor Kelly."

"I'll go, too," Alex instantly offered.

"No, you won't," Steve barked. "You'll stay right here with me and get the next shot set up. We'll work around Mickey and Kelly. Lisa, you drive. Here are the keys. Amy, give her the directions."

"But it's an emergency," Alex protested. "I think I should go . . ."

"It's a minor emergency," Steve barked. "Get back to work."

Steve leaned in the back window as Lisa slid into the driver's seat. "Mickey, feeling any better?"

"Don't worry, I won't get any blood on your car." Mickey saluted. "Better get back to work. The show must go on, as we say." Steve thumped on the door as the car pulled away. Kelly suspected he would call his lawyer the instant they were out of sight.

"I guess you'd better prepare for a long wait," she told Mickey. "You know how hospital emergency rooms are."

But two orderlies were ready with a wheel-chair as Lisa pulled up next to the emergency room entrance.

"My third movie star of the season!" one of the orderlies said, helping Mickey into the wheel-chair.

"Hey, I can walk."

"We can't be too careful," the orderly insisted.

"Kelly, do you think we should go back to the house and come back later to pick up Mickey?" Lisa asked.

"Kelly stays," Mickey said firmly. In the end, Lisa went back alone to help Steve out at the mansion.

Once they were inside the hospital, they were directed to the admissions desk. A matronly redheaded nurse gave Mickey the once-over and took out a sheaf of forms.

"Name, local address, and social security number, please," she said crisply, pointing at the proper blanks.

"Is all this really necessary?" Kelly asked. "Mickey's leg needs to be sewn up; it's bleeding. Couldn't he do this later?"

"Everyone has to fill out the forms first," the nurse snapped.

"Don't you know who this is?" Kelly's patience gave out completely. "This is Mickey Pines, the movie star. He doesn't need to fill out these dumb forms."

"The President of the United States has to fill out these 'dumb' forms," the redheaded nurse said coolly. "Name, address, social security number." She thrust the papers at Mickey.

Mickey grasped a pen and began writing. "No problem," he told Kelly. He looked up and gave the nurse his best little-boy grin. "Some of my favorite fans are redheaded nurses, you know."

"Well, I did take my niece to your last picture," the woman confessed. "She loved it. Say, do you mind telling me how much you get for one of those movies?"

"Too much." Mickey winked and filled in the rest of the insurance information.

"He needs medical attention, not questions about his salary," Kelly said testily.

"And who are you, another movie star?" The nurse glared. "I don't think I've ever seen you in the movies, honey, so you can just be patient, like everyone else."

The woman took Mickey's completed forms and beckoned to a young blond nurse. "Miss Hanson will show you to the examining room."

"Aren't you Mickey Pines?" Miss Hanson took Mickey's arm, stepping right in front of Kelly. "You're one of my favorite actors."

"Well, some of my favorite fans are blond nurses," Mickey said smoothly. Kelly's lips formed a hard, even line. He used the same lines on everybody, and they all fell for it! It was a pretty dirty trick, but somehow, when Mickey did it, she forgave him.

"Sit on the table. Dr. Felson will be right in." Miss Hanson smiled warmly at Mickey and left the room. Kelly heard her conversation with another nurse outside in the corridor.

"Wasn't that Mickey Pines, from the movies?"

"Yes, and he's a real doll," Miss Hanson answered.

"How about the girl? Is she anybody?"

"Nobody I know."

Mickey stretched out on the hospital gurney and closed his eyes, sighing deeply.

"That's better," Kelly said soothingly. "You always need rest after an accident; it's the shock of it, you know . . ."

"Hey—who's in charge here?" The doctor, whose tag read DR. FELSON, entered the room breezily. He clapped Kelly on the back and winked. "You happen to be right, but I get paid to tell him that. Now, let's take a look. You might want to wait outside," he said to Kelly. "Unless you like to watch while someone gets stitched back together."

"I'm going," she said hurriedly.

For the next few minutes, Kelly stood guard at the door. She wasn't exactly bothered by the envious stares and whispers of the hospital staff who thought she was Mickey's girlfriend. All in all, except for the fact that Mickey was injured, she had to admit she was enjoying herself.

"He's all yours." Dr. Felson held the door open and Mickey hopped through. "Sure you won't take the cane I offered?"

Mickey shook his head resolutely. "I hate canes. I'll manage on my own." Nevertheless, Mickey leaned on Kelly's shoulder.

"You're not a very good patient," Kelly scolded lightly.

"I hate being sick. I'm bored stiff already."

"Just make sure you stay off that leg for a while, and take the pills I gave you," Dr. Felson ordered. "And one more thing. While you're here, would you mind signing autographs in the children's wing?"

Mickey rolled his eyes, but Kelly could see he was pleased. "The sacrifices of being a star," he complained cheerfully. "Come on, Kelly, let's light up a few young lives."

A cheer went up as they pushed through the swinging doors into the children's wing.

So this is what it's like to be a movie star, Kelly thought. *I like it, I think.*

"Miss, miss." A small boy tugged at her jacket. "Can I have your autograph, too?"

"I'm not anyone famous."

"That's all right."

"Holding up all right?" Mickey asked her, amused at the group of children begging for Kelly's autograph.

"It's a little overwhelming. You know, Mickey, considering how people fuss over you, it's remarkable how natural you are."

Mickey raised an eyebrow. "Well, thanks for the compliment, but you're the one who's remarkable."

Mickey Pines was turning out to be quite a guy. Alex had definitely misjudged him, and the next time she saw Alex, she would tell him so—if they were still speaking, that is.

* * *

Kelly called the mansion and talked to Steve before they left the hospital. Then she called a cab.

"Your orders are to go straight to the Hampton Beach Hotel for a good rest. Steve booked a room for you," she told Mickey as they waited for the cab to arrive. "You're to stay on the Island tonight, instead of going back to the city. Steve seems very anxious that you give the leg a chance to heal."

"He's very anxious that I not quit the shoot, you mean," Mickey said. "Sure, I'll go to the hotel."

"Steve also said I have to go right back to Windward Point. I'm sorry, Mickey," Kelly said sincerely. "I wish I could hang around and cheer you up."

"Yeah, well, you can't have everything. Maybe I'll try to get some sleep." A horn honked outside, and Kelly helped Mickey to hobble out to the cab.

The ride to the hotel was short. Kelly helped Mickey to his room.

"I'll call you later," she promised, "to see how you're feeling."

"Without you, I won't be feeling too good."

"Wow," Kelly murmured as soon as she was back in the cab. " 'Without you, I won't be feeling too good.' Wait till I tell Jennifer about this!"

Seven

Back in the mansion's library, the next shot had already been set up, and Kelly was whisked through hair, makeup, and wardrobe. Lisa explained that all the clothes for the shot were by American designers who specialized in the nineteen forties look.

"I love this dress," Kelly told Lisa. "I used to be self-conscious about my shoulders because they're so broad. But now I love clothes that emphasize my shoulders."

She examined herself in the mirror, pleased by the effect of the sophisticated dress. It really was stunning. The arms and shoulders of the dress were made of sheer netting, and were dotted with hundreds of tiny gold bugle beads. It gave the illusion of sparkling bareness. The rest of the dress was made of gold lamé, which defined every curve of her body.

"Put these on." Lisa gave her a pair of short, tight gloves in the exact shade of gold as the dress. But the finishing touch was a turban: an exotic creation of gold lamé, which was gathered and fastened in the front. Kelly noticed that the gold color really brought out the blue in her eyes. *When Alex sees me in this outfit, he won't think I'm so naive,* she thought.

The Kendalls appeared, looking, Kelly had to admit, quite impressive and regal in their cocktail clothes.

Sir Ernest headed straight for Maxi, who was brilliant herself in a deep red, tightly fitted suit and matching hat. Kelly had a pang of jealousy over the hat, since she'd hoped her turban would be the only headpiece.

But as Maxi allowed Sir Ernest to kiss her hand, Kelly saw the tall brunette's eyes move, searching for another person in the room.

"Alex, set those reflectors farther back; they show in the frame," Steve said, peering through the camera.

Alex hoisted one of the white panels and lifted it easily to a side wall.

"You must be very strong," Maxi simpered. Kelly almost laughed; Alex hated women who came on too strong.

"This is nothing," he boasted. "The photo equipment is the really heavy stuff. Try moving that around all day."

Kelly couldn't believe her ears. She did her best to ignore the two of them.

"Something's wrong with this shot—it doesn't work for me," Steve complained. "What do you think, Marilyn? Is it what you had in mind in your layout?"

Marilyn frowned. "This is supposed to be a nineteen forties cocktail party," she explained, "the kind where the superrich get together to raise money for war bonds. The Kendalls are the wealthy host and hostess, and Kelly is supposed to be a spy. She slips a sedative into Fiona's drink while Sir Ernest is busy flirting with Maxi. It's supposed to be funny and very stylized, a clip from a forties movie. But this is dull, Steve. Dull, dull, dull."

"It's the couch," Alex blurted out. Steve gave him a warning look. He didn't like his assistants to offer their opinions without being asked. But Marilyn seemed interested.

"What about the couch?" she demanded.

"It's too dead center; everyone looks lined up like chess pieces or something. If you angle the couch, you can have two groups of action; Sir Ernest and Maxi to the back, Kelly and Lady Kendall in front."

"But the clothes—they have to be the focus of attention," Lisa, ever the stylist, reminded him.

"They will be if Maxi sits on the back of the sofa." Alex demonstrated, hopping up and swinging one leg along the sofa back. "Get the idea?

And you'll still see all of Sir Ernest's suit if he stands a little to the side, like this."

Marilyn broke into the biggest smile Kelly had yet seen on the art director's usually dour face. "You're right. That works perfectly! Steve, where do you find these talented assistants?"

"They seem to find me," Steve said grumpily.

As Alex and Lisa pushed the couch into the position he had suggested, Kelly noticed how Maxi's eyes followed Alex's every move.

"That was *such* a good idea," she whispered in a disgustingly phony voice as Alex stood back to see how the scene looked. Instead of ignoring her, Alex looped his arm around Maxi's waist, making sure Kelly was watching as he whispered something into Maxi's ear. The slim brunette giggled out loud.

"Places, people," Steve barked. "We're running late."

Quickly, Maxi draped herself along the back of the couch, casting sultry glances at Alex the whole time.

"Look at Sir Ernest," Steve directed her. "Come on, you're trying to seduce the old guy."

"Like this?" Maxi gave a seductive glance— right to Alex!

Fuming, Kelly turned away, concentrating on her role in the shot as the sneaky spy poisoning Fiona's drink.

If Alex is trying to make me jealous, he'll have to try pretty hard, she thought, tossing her head arrogantly. *Flirting with Maxi, indeed. As if I care one way or the other what Alex does. He can have Maxi, as far as I'm concerned. I have absolutely no interest in Alex at all . . .*

"My dear," Lady Kendall exclaimed, grasping Kelly's arm, "I know you're supposed to be a spy, but that look on your face is enough to frighten me to death! Do you have to look so angry?"

A male voice interrupted Fiona's words. "Who's angry?"

"Mickey!" Kelly cried, positively delighted to see him. "What are you doing here? The doctor told you to keep off that leg."

"I couldn't sleep and it's pretty boring in that hotel. Hey, nice hat," he said, eyeing her appreciatively.

"Thanks. Glad you like it." Mickey didn't even notice that Maxi had on a hat, too!

Mickey inspected her turban. "What's that thing for, anyway?" he teased. "To keep your hair from falling off?"

Everyone laughed, even Steve. "Okay, Mickey—these people have work to do," he said. "Let's try a shot of this scene."

Eagerly, Kelly took her place, this time grinning devilishly as she pretended to slip the poison capsule into Fiona's drink.

"That's the spirit," Steve called. "Hold it . . . Great! Terrific shot! Mickey—guess we needed a spot of life to get this shot off the ground. Maybe you should stick around for the rest of this layout."

"That's exactly what I had in mind," Mickey said, grinning in Kelly's direction.

They finished the pose in record time.

"Alex, strike the set," Steve ordered, clapping Mickey on the shoulder. "If you ever think of going into the photography business, let me know. You have a real knack with people."

"I have my work cut out for me already," Mickey answered, laughing.

Kelly hurried over. "It did help, having you here watching."

"Actually, the real reason I came over was to take you out to dinner. How about it? I can't stand eating alone in that crummy hotel."

"I—I can't," Kelly cried, stricken. "You know I have that hired car coming to take me back to New Jersey."

"But this is a special circumstance—I'm injured, remember? You can send the car back and I'll get you home afterward."

"But, Mickey, I told you," she faltered, "my family . . ."

"Okay, don't make me beg. I know when I'm licked."

"Believe me, Mickey, I'd have dinner with you if I could. There's just no way."

"Well, I hate to think of you going to waste like this every night," he said lightly.

"Maybe I could arrange something for tomorrow night," Kelly said.

"Hey, no big deal—maybe another time, okay?"

"I'd really like that, Mickey."

Amy interrupted. "Better get changed, Kelly. I've got to get these clothes back tonight."

Kelly trudged up the stairs to the dressing room, crushed by disappointment. Another time, Mickey had said—but what if there never was another time? Life was so unfair.

The stunning dress fell to the floor in a heap and Kelly nearly left it there. She had no use for fancy dresses now. But out of loyalty to Amy, she picked it up and put it on a hanger. Then she pulled on her sweater, her tired jeans, and her worn-out, broken-down boots and yanked her jacket on. The hired car was already waiting outside. She climbed in, grunting at the driver's friendly greeting. She felt like a schoolgirl who has detention while everyone else gets to go to a party.

If life were perfect, she'd be getting into a waiting limo with Mickey, wearing the gold lamé dress, making a grand entrance on Mickey's arm to some fabulous restaurant. Oh, why was she a high-school junior? If only she was older, an independent college girl, without parents nagging her about homework! The shoot would be the most romantic time of her entire life.

Kelly's mood hadn't improved by the time she got home, so she wasn't thrilled when Tina and her mother ambushed her inside the door.

"How did the shoot go?" Tina asked eagerly. "What was it like? How was Mickey? Is he as cute in person as in the movies?"

"Honey, where's Alex?" her mother asked, looking past Kelly. "Didn't he come with you?"

"No. Our plans changed. I came home by limo. And the shoot was fine. Everyone was great." She didn't want to tell her mother what she thought of snobbish Fiona or lecherous Sir Ernest.

"Ha," Tina snorted. "Listen to her. I'll bet you were falling over your feet today, you were so excited about this job."

"I wasn't all that excited, Tina," she said scornfully. "I've seen famous people before."

"You have not," Tina cried indignantly, "not up close, anyway."

"I've met designers and photographers and famous models, haven't I?" Her voice rose in frustration.

"You must be hungry," Mrs. Blake said soothingly. "You always get cranky when you're tired or hungry. I'll get your dinner."

"I'm not *cranky*," Kelly exploded. "I'm not a baby, you know. I'm sixteen years old and professionally employed and making enough money to send myself to college—and Tina, too, I hope. But you still treat me like a child! I had to turn down dinner with Mickey Pines tonight because I had to come home and do my *homework*. It was *humiliating*!"

"Kelly! her mother cried.

"Mickey Pines asked you to dinner?" Tina gasped, clutching her chest. "I don't believe it!"

Kelly fled up the stairs. "You don't understand anything," she yelled. "You don't even care!"

Minutes later, her mother knocked firmly on Kelly's door.

"Go away," she ordered tearfully. "I don't want to talk to you."

"Don't you speak to me that way, young lady. Meg Dorian is on the phone—I told her I'd get you, but then you'd better be ready to have a talk with me."

Meg. What could she want? Did I do something wrong today without realizing it? Wiping her eyes, Kelly picked up the telephone.

"Kelly, how was your first day?" Meg asked.

"Fine, just fine." Then she hadn't done anything wrong.

"Good, good. I knew you'd enjoy this assignment. I have big news. I happen to know," Meg said slyly, "that a reporter for *Celebrity* magazine will be at the mansion tomorrow to do a piece about Mickey Pines. It will be fabulous exposure for you. We'll make you as much of a celebrity as any movie star! Now aren't you glad you didn't take the Greek Islands assignment? This is even better for your career! I have such big plans for you."

"That's—that's great," Kelly stammered, a bit overwhelmed. She'd fantasized about photos of herself with Mickey, and now the fantasy would come true!

"Kelly—are you there?" Meg's no-nonsense voice brought her back to earth.

"I'm here."

"Make sure you get plenty of sleep tonight. I want you looking fresh. I went to a lot of trouble to arrange this 'coincidence,' so don't let me down. This is important."

"I won't let you down," Kelly assured her. "And thanks, Meg."

When she'd hung up the phone, Kelly sat in thought for a few minutes. Then she went back downstairs.

"What did Meg want?" her mother asked when Kelly entered the kitchen.

"There's going to be a reporter from *Celebrity* magazine at the shoot tomorrow. Meg arranged it so I could get more exposure."

"I see," Mrs. Blake said thoughtfully.

"Do you, Mom? Do you see why I have to be treated more like an adult? A reporter from a famous magazine is interviewing me tomorrow, movie stars are asking me for dates, and you're still acting like I'm a child. I'm not your little girl anymore, Mom, and you can't protect me from life. It's time for you to let go a little."

"You're only sixteen, Kelly."

"That's old enough to make some decisions for myself. You know what Meg says—exposure is important to my career. Having dinner with Mickey Pines tonight would've been fabulous exposure, and I should've gone. But I had to say no."

Mrs. Blake frowned. "I'm not sure I want you to live that kind of life. It . . . it doesn't sound wholesome."

"Mom, can't you trust me a little? You've spent sixteen years raising me. If you haven't done the job by now, you might as well give up!"

Her mother sighed. "Everything is happening so fast. . . . Exactly what do you want me to say, Kelly?"

"Well, I probably won't ever get another dinner invitation like I did tonight, but if I did—I just want to make the decision myself. I'll know if I can handle it or not. Please?"

Mrs. Blake's scowl softened. "I guess you've always been sensible. You do go overboard sometimes, but I suppose you'll outgrow that."

"Then you admit I'm sensible."

"Yes, but . . . It's such a fast life. Movie stars, publicity. I don't feel exactly comfortable with it."

"But I do," Kelly said quickly. "I really can handle it, Mom. I know I can."

Her mother gave her a searching look. "Maybe you're right. Sometimes I think you're more worldly than I'll ever be. Okay, Kelly, you win."

"Fantastic," Kelly squealed. "Thanks, Mom . . ."

"Hold on! This doesn't mean you can go wild."

"I won't," Kelly promised. "I'll be very responsible."

"And I still expect you to talk things over with me, and your dad." Suddenly Mrs. Blake looked crestfallen. "I can't believe you're so grown up, so soon . . ."

"Oh, Mom," Kelly groaned. "I've got to call Jen before I eat, okay?"

Kelly rushed upstairs and dialed her best friend's number in record time.

"Jen," she yelled before Jennifer could even say hello, "have I got news for you!" Hurriedly, she told her everything that had happened that day, ending with her mother's decision to let her be more responsible for herself.

"Do you realize what this means?" she added, practically out of breath. "I may get another chance to go out with Mickey!"

"Tomorrow is already Friday," Jennifer said, as predictably sensible as ever. "I wouldn't count on it if I were you—he probably has plans for the weekend."

"Oh Jen, what if you're right? What if he's jetting to Paris or something?"

"I read that he doesn't have a steady girl-friend," Jennifer said helpfully. "Maybe he'll call you some other time."

"He'll forget me if I don't go out with him now. I guess I could ask *him* out—maybe for Saturday. Help me think of a plan . . ."

"Saturday? Don't you have a date with Eric?"

"Eric! I totally forgot!" She felt a chill go through her; this was the first time since he'd moved across the street that she hadn't spied on

Eric's house the minute she got in, to see if he was home or—horror of horrors—out with another girl. "You know, Jen, things really *are* happening fast in my life if I can forget about Eric for five minutes!"

"It's amazing," Jennifer agreed. "But I guess you'd forget about anyone when a movie star asks you out!"

"But I've never done that before. Even when I started going out with Alex, I still liked Eric better."

"You're loyal," Jennifer said simply. "Most girls would've dumped Eric for Alex, you know. Alex is older and a lot more sophisticated."

"What are you saying? That I shouldn't feel guilty about forgetting Eric?"

Jennifer considered the question. "You don't really owe Eric anything," she finally said, "since you're not seeing each other exclusively. If I were you, I'd worry more about Alex getting jealous. After all, he's right there. You'd be dating some-one else right under his nose!"

Kelly scoffed. "Alex is having a grand time with Maxi Bond, one of the other models."

"Alex?" Jennifer was surprised. "I thought he didn't like models—except you, of course."

"Well, he likes one now, or at least he's acting like he does. To tell you the truth, Jen"—she giggled—"I think he's just trying to make me jealous."

"Sure, because you're making him jealous with Mickey Pines! Every girl should have your problems," Jennifer sighed enviously. "Three men after you at once—and one of them a movie star."

"I won't have anyone after me at all if I don't watch out," Kelly admitted. "Alex has resigned himself to my crush on Eric, or so he says, but going out with Mickey could be risky."

"You're right," Jennifer agreed. "You could wind up with no one if you're not careful. So the logical, reasonable thing for you to do is to forget all about Mickey, make up with Alex, and keep your date with Eric."

"Jen, you're absolutely right."

"Then you're going to do it?"

They answered the question in unison: "Absolutely not!"

Eight

Kelly held up a large mirror and smiled at her reflection. "Thanks, Pepe, the hairdo's wonderful. And Oliver's makeup is terrific, of course."

Privately she was thinking, *this morning was certainly a waste*. She'd spent hours watching Cheri, Maxi, and the Kendalls work on a group shot: not exactly her idea of fun.

Amy was waiting as she left the makeup area. "You look fabulous!" the editor exclaimed, admiring Kelly's outfit for that afternoon's setup: an oversize cashmere sweater and a calf-length wool skirt. The setting for the scene was the nineteen fifties.

"Fabulous?" Kelly lifted a sweatered arm and cringed. "Ugh, this is so hot! Why do I have to wear this while Cheri and Maxi got to slink around in those formals all morning?"

"Who cares how good Cheri or Maxi looked this morning?" Amy countered. "No one important was there to see them." She winked, then held up a hand to stifle a big yawn. "Mickey will be back for the shoot this afternoon, and I absolutely guarantee that you'll be happy with the way you look."

"I am happy," Kelly told her, "but you look exhausted. Everyone does. I'm almost glad I was just watching."

"After partying all night, you'd look exhausted, too."

"Partying? What party? Why didn't anyone say anything about it this morning?"

"No one said anything because Steve was furious we all looked so tired. Don't worry, you didn't miss much. It was fun, but no big social event. Last night after you'd left I was packing up, getting ready to go, when Cheri insisted we all go out. Well, all except Franklyn and Rebecca—they went off by themselves. See, Cheri was supposed to have dinner with Mickey alone, but the Kendalls somehow invited themselves along, so Cheri . . ."

Kelly's cheeks were burning. "Cheri and Mickey had a date last night?"

"Yes, and Sir Ernest tried to horn in on it. Cheri was fuming."

"I don't blame her," Kelly muttered.

"Cheri can't stand Sir Ernest, and she figured

her only chance to dump him and Fiona was to gather a big crowd, so she could give the Kendalls the slip."

"Very sensible," Kelly said dryly. "And did she give them the slip?"

"Sort of."

"Then Cheri got to be alone with Mickey?"

"If you call being in a room with fifty other people alone. Mickey sure loves attention—he had everyone in the restaurant gathered around our table while he did scenes from his movies. What a show-off."

What have I done? I should have lied through my teeth to stay last night. So Mickey asked Cheri to dinner when I couldn't go. But did he really want to be alone with Cheri, or was he looking for company because I couldn't be there?

"I guess no one likes to eat alone," she said, hoping Amy would fill in any details, but Amy only nodded, stifling another yawn.

Kelly's good mood was fading fast. She'd imagined Mickey would be eager to see her today, but maybe she was wrong. *If I get another invitation from him, I'll snap at it this time! Have I already been replaced by Cheri?*

"You must have stayed out pretty late," Kelly said as Amy helped her adjust the skirt and sweater.

"I'll say. We all went disco hopping, except Mickey, of course. He left after dinner. With that leg, he couldn't do any dancing, and the painkillers the doctor gave him made him drowsy. He missed a great time. Southampton has some real hot spots. Arlene, Alex, Lisa, and I didn't get back to the city until three this morning. I'm barely awake. I'll never do that on a work night again!"

"No, you shouldn't do that on a work night," Kelly agreed. So Mickey had gone back to his hotel. He'd asked Cheri to dinner, but he'd gone back to the hotel right afterward. That was a good sign.

She peered at herself in the mirror. Ankle socks and flats, hardly the kind of outfit that interested a man.

"You look terrific," Amy assured her. "Just add a smile and you'll be irresistible, I promise."

"A smile and ankle socks," Kelly scoffed. "No offense, but they're not exactly a winning combination."

When she entered the big brick carriage house, Alex, looking as tired as Amy, glanced at her sharply. Kelly shivered; the converted building that now housed an extensive collection of nineteen fifties cars was unheated. She would have gone right back to the mansion for her jacket, but Steve, overtired and irritable, was barking commands at everyone. The last thing Kelly wanted was to draw attention to herself. When Steve was in a foul mood, it was best to stay out of his way.

"Your boyfriend was the life of the party last

night." Alex sidled over to Kelly, a smug look on his face. "Too bad *you* weren't invited. Mickey and Cheri had a great time, and so did Maxi and I."

"I'm sure you did," Kelly said archly. "And I'm glad you all kept Mickey amused. He was so upset I couldn't stay to dinner with him that I suggested he ask Cheri to keep him company. It's no fun being alone when you're recuperating."

"You told Mickey to ask Cheri out?"

"Well, I felt terrible that I couldn't stay with him," she said truthfully enough. "He wasn't feeling his best after the accident."

Alex's smug look had disappeared. "Oh. Well, I guess Cheri took his mind off his pain. He seemed to enjoy himself all right."

"But he went home early," Kelly pointed out. "Mickey doesn't really care for large crowds. I'm sure he would have preferred a quiet dinner with me."

"Oh, yeah? He gives a great imitation of a party animal." Alex chuckled slyly. "He's a pretty wild guy, Kelly. I hope you can keep up with him."

"Don't worry about it," she said coolly. "I'm sure I can keep up with anything Mickey has in mind."

"If you get the chance," Alex taunted. "Our boy might be interested in a new victim."

"I told you," she insisted. "He only dated Cheri because I couldn't be there. Mickey's really very different."

"He is, huh? My guess is, he told you exactly what he thought you wanted to hear."

"Not everyone is as clever as you, Alex. Maybe that's what you would have done in his place, but Mickey Pines is honest."

"The real Mickey," Alex said sarcastically.

"Yes, the Mickey I liked. The Mickey I will continue to like."

"Then how do you explain this sensitive loner suddenly becoming the life of the party? He didn't want to be alone last night."

"Oh, this is silly, Alex. Everyone needs some excitement from time to time. Stop making a big deal out of nothing!"

"It's the truth, Kelly, and if you weren't so stubborn you'd admit it. Mickey Pines is handing you a line. He's not what you think he is."

"He's not what *you* think he is, either," she declared.

"Hey, man, dig this crazy garage!" With a wide grin, Mickey swaggered into the carriage house; he was a juvenile delinquent, fifties style, but an elegant one with his short suede jacket, matching gloves, and richly colored sweater over skin-tight jeans.

His blond hair had been styled in an exaggerated Elvis pompadour that flopped in his eyes, and everyone laughed as he grasped an imaginary microphone and swiveled his hips, just like Elvis.

"Mickey, you look much better today," Kelly called brightly, for Alex's benefit. To her satisfaction, Mickey hurried to her side, limping only slightly, and put a friendly arm around her shoulders.

"I couldn't disappoint my loyal coworkers." He grinned. "What's a little pain, anyway?"

The smile he gave her was so sweet her heart melted.

So what if he'd showed off last night? Mickey's funny and people love him because he makes them laugh. There's nothing wrong with that.

She gave him an admiring look, and he answered it with a friendly squeeze. "So how's my favorite doctor this morning?"

"I'm fine," she said, putting her arm around his waist. Alex glowered at them. "And you really do look great. Getting out last night did you good. Your leg seems much better."

Mickey gave her another squeeze, and Alex marched over to a corner to check a spotlight.

"I feel terrific," Mickey said. "But you're shivering. Where's your coat?"

"I left it inside. I didn't realize it would be so cold out here."

Mickey tightened both arms around her. "No problem. I'll keep you warm."

"Perfect," called an unfamiliar voice. Kelly looked up in surprise. A skinny young man loaded down with camera gear was standing nearby. Behind him, a woman scribbled notes in a reporter's notebook before extending a hand to Mickey. "Elsa Simmons and Tim Ross, from *Celebrity* magazine. That's just the kind of angle we need—Mickey interacting with the other folks here."

Kelly had nearly forgotten about the publicity piece, and from the look on Steve's face, he wasn't too thrilled to be sharing his models with the popular magazine.

"We won't get in your way," Elsa promised Steve. "No photos till they're out of their wardrobe, and we won't show the mansion, either. Just tell us where to stand and we'll be as unobtrusive as possible."

But they were obtrusive, asking questions at the worst possible moments. Finally Steve threw up his hands in exasperation. "Look, just ask all the questions you want and then get out of here. I've got an assignment to shoot and we're way behind schedule already."

"But, Steve . . ." Kelly said hesitantly. "We'll have to change for Tim to photograph us. The magazine would never allow these fashions to be scooped."

"Fine, change!" Steve snapped. "It's clear that we'll get nothing done till these people are gone."

Kelly and Mickey changed their clothes hastily upstairs.

"Where's Steve's sense of humor?" Mickey asked when they were back in the carriage house. "We're not that far behind schedule."

"Steve takes it out on everyone when he loses control."

"Well, don't worry. I'll protect you from his nasty temper." Mickey tousled Kelly's hair fondly.

Kelly couldn't help gloating; there'd be pictures of her with Mickey Pines in a national magazine. Things were going splendidly.

She led Tim and Elsa down to the beach. The reporters began to snap pictures and ask questions; Mickey made a big show of keeping Kelly warm, teasing and cracking jokes. Kelly was in seventh heaven from all the attention. Yet she couldn't help noticing that Mickey fussed over her most when Tim's camera was pointed his way.

But it's silly to criticize. Publicity's important to Mickey's career. And Meg arranged this whole thing for my benefit, too. I'm as guilty of publicity-seeking as Mickey, if not more, she reminded herself.

"Are you used to working with movie stars?" Elsa asked her.

"Well, no—actually, this is the first time that I . . ."

"Have you seen all of Mickey's movies?"

"Yes, my little sister makes me go to every one and I . . ."

"Is Mickey easy to get along with?"

"Very, in fact I . . ."

Elsa turned her back on Kelly. "I notice you're limping slightly," she said to Mickey. "Is something wrong?"

Mickey told the story of his injury with a flourish, and Elsa ate it up. "That's a fantastic angle—the celluloid hero being rescued for once, instead of coming to the rescue. Let's get a shot of Kelly carrying Mickey on those rocks where it happened."

Tim suggested they pose against the rocks and crashing waves. "Mickey, you lean against Kelly, and hold out that bandaged leg. Perfect . . . hold it . . ."

At the last minute, Mickey suddenly scooped Kelly up in his arms. Tim's shutter clicked, capturing Kelly's very startled face and Mickey's grinning one.

"My fans would be upset if I let a woman rescue me," he quipped lightly.

"Maybe so," Kelly spluttered, "but I did rescue you, and I don't especially like to be picked up that way."

"Oh, come on, it's just for fun," Elsa cajoled. "It will be an adorable picture."

"An adorable picture of me looking helpless. I'd rather we did another one," Kelly protested.

Mickey seemed annoyed. "When you're famous, we'll think about how you look, okay?"

She was shocked and hurt, and knew her red face showed it.

"You're taking it too seriously," Mickey told her, lifting her chin. "Come on, this is a stupid thing to fight about." He looked like a naughty little boy, abashed and boastful at the same time—it was almost impossible to be angry with him.

"Oh, maybe you're right," she said, suddenly uncertain. Maybe she *had* overreacted. Mickey was a star, and after all, she was a virtual unknown. "I—I guess I shouldn't have made such a fuss," she murmured, and Mickey rewarded her with a kiss on the lips that took her breath away. She wished Elsa and Tim weren't there—how was she ever going to get to know this intriguing guy when they were constantly surrounded by crowds of people?

By the time Elsa and Tim finished and Kelly and Mickey had changed back into their clothes for the shoot, Steve was fuming.

"It's about time," he snapped angrily. "I hope you still remember how to work, Kelly. We haven't got all day."

"Hey, there's no need to be rude to the lady," Mickey snapped back. "You'll get plenty of business if this publicity helps Kelly's career, so lay off."

That stopped Steve cold, and for the next few minutes they all worked quickly and efficiently— and silently. Even Lisa and Alex were subdued. Kelly found herself wishing that Alex would do something to ease the tension—he'd always been good at calming Steve's moods. But Alex wouldn't even look at her. She wasn't used to working in almost total silence, and she felt self-conscious without the usual cheerful banter on the set.

The art director was the only one who didn't seem to mind the tension. "Don't forget that special car shot," Marilyn said. "You'll have to move the Oldsmobile out in front."

She showed Steve the layout for the photo, which would feature Kelly behind the wheel and Mickey on the running board of the old automobile.

"I'll do it." Alex slid behind the wheel and turned the starter key. The engine sputtered, choked, and died. He tried again, this time letting out the clutch and shifting gears expertly. There was a horrible grinding sound, but the car refused to start.

"Oh, great—another disaster," Steve snarled.

"It must be cold," Alex retorted. "I'll try again in a minute. The worst thing would be to flood the engine."

"It might be something else," Mickey suggested quietly. "The solenoid, or the carburetor . . ."

"I think I know as much about cars as you do." Alex's eyes flashed, but he lifted the hood and poked around inside.

Kelly felt a stab of embarrassment for Alex when, after he'd tinkered under the hood for ten minutes, the car still refused to start. Steve had lost all patience.

"Forget the shot," he exploded. "We'll do something else."

"That shot is very important," Marilyn said indignantly. "I can't change the layout now, everything has been approved. Push the car! Do something! I need that shot!"

"It's okay," Mickey said, interrupting before a real battle developed. "I think I can help. Alex—hand me your jacket so I don't ruin these designer duds."

Reluctantly, Alex took off his jacket and Mickey disappeared under the hood, muttering to himself.

"Try it now," he called.

Alex turned the key and the engine burst into life. "Oh. Well, I guess it finally warmed up," he said lamely.

"Thank goodness someone around here knows about cars," Marilyn snapped. "Now let's get the shot."

Mickey returned Alex's jacket. "Hey, don't feel bad, Alex—you couldn't have known how to fix it. My old man had one of these cars for years. He was so cheap he wouldn't trade it in. In fact, I think he still uses it, with a special license from the Antique Car Owner's Association."

Steve and Lisa and even Marilyn chuckled, but Alex's face grew red and stayed that way as he drove the car into place.

"That was a nice thing to do," Kelly told Mickey, "trying to make Alex feel better. He wasn't very nice to you."

Mickey shrugged bashfully. "No big deal," he muttered.

"Okay, people, no more breaks today," Steve announced. "As soon as we finish this shot, we'll move on to the observatory scene. We've wasted enough time. I think we can finish the last shots if we keep going."

"He's so worried about that party scene," Amy said to Kelly. "Everyone's in it, and the group shots can be real traumatic."

Their last shot! Kelly was filled with dismay. The assignment was almost over and she'd had no chance to be alone with Mickey, or even to find out where she stood with him.

Last night everything seemed to be going so well. But now . . . if something doesn't happen soon, I may as well forget about Mickey. It was depressing.

Nine

The glassed-in observatory sparkled like an opened jewel box as flashes of light from the spotlights and reflectors arranged around the floor bounced off the glass. Kelly, glamorous in a body-skimming silver jumpsuit, gasped in delight when she stepped from the mansion's tiny elevator into the impressive room. Everyone was there for the final group shot: the Kendalls, Franklyn Deeds and Rebecca Halloway, Maxi, Cheri, and, of course, Mickey.

"It's magnificent," Kelly said, as awed by the sparkling outfits of the assembled cast as by the soaring domed roof and the huge telescope aimed at the night sky.

"Something else is magnificent." Mickey was at

her side, and his appreciative glance left no doubt he was referring to her.

Kelly blushed with pleasure. Cheri and Maxi, wearing variations of the same formfitting jumpsuit, looked equally stunning, but Mickey didn't seem to notice them at all.

"Thanks, I'm glad you like it." Her eyes seemed to lock into his; she felt she could stand there, just looking at him, forever. She couldn't let him slip away. How could she say good-bye to her one chance to be in love with a movie star?

"Mickey," she faltered, "um, maybe tonight . . ."

"Mickey, darling!" Fiona Kendall, surprisingly chic and youthful in a metallic-looking tunic over shiny stretch pants, neatly shoved Kelly aside, lacing her arm through Mickey's. "Mickey, dear, you were simply *marvelous* company last night. I do hope you'll allow me to reciprocate. Perhaps we could share some champagne in your room tonight?"

Mickey gently disentangled his arm from hers. "Aren't you sweet," he said evenly, "but I've already made plans for this evening. I'll be very busy."

Plans for this evening! Kelly was suddenly sure that Mickey's plans included Cheri. He certainly hadn't made any that included Kelly!

Fiona, meanwhile, turned and strode away.

"Sorry, Kelly." Mickey grinned. "The trials of being a star. What were you saying?"

"Just that I hope this shoot doesn't last too long

tonight. Everyone seems to have . . . special plans."

Mickey frowned. "What have you got planned?"

Kelly colored fiercely. To think she had almost embarrassed herself by asking Mickey if he had a date! "Who, me? Well, I thought . . ."

Luckily, Steve saved her from finishing her thoughts. "Okay, folks," he interrupted. Kelly breathed a sigh of relief and turned to listen to Steve.

"Pay attention. First we're going to do individual shots of our celebrities with the telescope, stars gazing at stars. Mickey, come over here, this is your mark for the first shot."

Kelly stepped to one side and found herself standing next to Cheri—the last person she wanted to talk to.

"The Kendalls have no shame," Cheri said to Kelly under her breath. "She and Sir Ernest really deserve each other. He was after me all last night, and Fiona was practically crawling over Mickey. They sure know how to spoil a fun evening."

"Oh, was it spoiled?" Kelly said lightly. "Well, I guess you'll get a second chance tonight."

Cheri frowned. "Tonight! What do you mean? I'm heading straight for my boyfriend's country place tonight."

"Your boyfriend," Kelly said weakly.

Cheri's eyes narrowed. "What's the matter? Did you think I couldn't get myself a boyfriend or something?"

"No, no, of course you'd have a boyfriend. I just thought—well, maybe you'd be going out with someone here tonight. Like, well . . ."

"Like Mickey Pines?" Cheri tossed her head. "Forget that scene—when I go out, I like to be the center of attention. Going out with Mickey Pines is like being somebody's baggage—no one pays any attention to you at all. I thought I'd get noticed, which wouldn't hurt my career any, but no dice. Mickey had center stage all night. I wouldn't go through that again even if he asked me!"

"Oh," Kelly said, relief flooding through her. "Oh, I guess someone like you wouldn't put up with that."

Cheri squinted her eyes again. "Hey, is that supposed to be an insult?"

Kelly was suddenly too happy to start a scene. "Of course not. I meant I know exactly how you feel." Kelly's mind was racing. So Cheri's plans didn't include Mickey after all. *Maybe he still likes me!*

"This will be your last pose, Mickey," Steve said happily. "You've sailed through like a real pro. Listen, if all the shots go this smoothly, we'll wrap early today."

Everyone applauded. "We'll do the Kendalls next," Steve continued. "Alex, get me some fresh film, will you please?"

Alex loaded the film into the camera while

Steve and Marilyn explained the kind of poses they wanted from Sir Ernest and Fiona.

"You mean something like this?" Sir Ernest froze, his expression a cartoon of a dashing hero, like something out of a silent movie.

"Uh, not exactly," Steve said. "Couldn't you do something more . . . relaxed?"

"Are you implying there is something wrong with my interpretation?" Sir Ernest answered in short, clipped tones.

Steve let out a long, slow breath. "Look, we're all getting tired, but if you'll just listen to what I say—"

"I beg your pardon!" Sir Ernest was livid. "Do I have no artistic judgment of my own?"

"Hey, hey, let's not squabble," Franklyn Deeds put in, making one of his rare comments. "We all have important things to do."

"Yeah, me too," Rebecca added.

Everyone started talking at once, blaming Sir Ernest for keeping them from important plans. The only one who seemed perfectly happy about it all was Maxi, whose big dark eyes were fixed on Alex the whole time.

"Everyone, simmer down!" Arlene called in desperation. "Look, there's plenty of food left from lunch—none of us seemed to be hungry today. Let's take a break. Maybe we'll all feel better after we eat something."

"Let's hope so," Marilyn muttered darkly.

But things didn't improve even after eating the picnic supper. Sir Ernest took forever with his shots, and Fiona gave Steve just as much trouble with hers. When Franklyn Deeds took his position at the telescope, things really went downhill.

"He must take lessons in being a pain," Kelly murmured to Arlene. "I've never seen anyone make such a fuss over one simple close-up."

"Tell me about it," Arlene groaned. "Every time Steve snaps the shutter, Franklyn has his mouth open. I never saw such perfect timing! He's ruined at least eight shots."

"And I never saw anyone so vain. No model insists on approving the Polaroids of every pose; that's what the art director is for. But Franklyn has to check that every precise hair is in place! If his fans knew how much makeup macho-man wears, they'd never go to see his movies again."

Rebecca Halloway was just as bad as Franklyn, and by the time they finally finished the close-ups, Steve's bad manners were at an all-time low. Marilyn and Arlene had their hands full, trying to keep tempers in check. Then, finally, it was time to do the group shots.

Kelly's outfit didn't include a watch, and she was beginning to be worried about the late hour. She didn't want her parents to start wondering where she was, especially after her talk with her mother about responsibility.

Steve used his aerial tripod for the final shot. By climbing to the top of a ladder, he was able to look down at the whole group as they raised champagne glasses filled with ginger ale.

"Lift the glasses and smile," Steve commanded glumly.

"Come on," Marilyn cried, "liven it up! You all look dead! This is supposed to be a party scene. Act happy. Look alive!"

"Try it again," Steve said. "Ready . . . raise your arms and smile."

"Ouch!" Cheri screamed at Fiona. "Your bracelet's caught in my hair! What are you trying to do, pull all my hair out?"

"Excuse me, I certainly didn't do it on purpose."

"This is pathetic," Steve groaned. "I've never seen such a hopeless bunch."

"You might try thanking us for the hard work we've done, instead of criticizing all the time," Franklyn yelled.

A chorus of approval greeted his remark. "He's right," Rebecca shouted.

"I quite agree," Fiona chimed in.

"People, people," Arlene cried. "Please, we're all in this together."

"Now look, my last frame is spoiled!" Steve threw his hands up in disgust.

Marilyn took control. "Look, it's nearly ten o'clock. Let's call it quits—we can't get any work done under these conditions. We'll have to finish up tomorrow morning."

Ten o'clock! Kelly thought, horrified.

"Tomorrow? I'll be in Connecticut tomorrow," Cheri cried. "I have plans. Believe me, I have better things to do than to hang around here one more day."

"We all had plans," Mickey said, trying to calm the group, but even he failed to lighten the mood.

"It's tomorrow or nothing," Marilyn snapped. "We'll just waste time if we try to finish tonight."

"She's right," Arlene said desperately. "You all need a break. You've been working terrifically hard. I'll book you the best rooms at the Hamptons Beach Hotel, and you can get a decent dinner from room service. After a good night's rest we'll be able to finish in no time in the morning. Cheri, I promise you, you'll get to Connecticut by lunchtime. We'll start shooting at the crack of dawn."

"Good heavens," Fiona cried in alarm, "I hope not."

"Okay, we'll start whenever you say." Arlene was desperate. "Please, you can't quit now. Think of all those disappointed fans—don't let your public down."

"Think of the generous bonus we're going to pay for overtime," Marilyn added cynically.

"Well, I think ten A.M. would be suitable," Fiona purred.

There were more complaints, but finally everyone agreed that ten o'clock was fine. They practically fell over each other as they raced for the dressing rooms to take off their makeup and give Lisa their outfits.

Kelly headed straight for the telephone.

"Mom, it's me. I know it's late, but I already told you we were running over schedule. . . . No, don't wait up for me because I'm not coming home. Wait a minute—we're all staying out here, at the Hamptons Beach Hotel. . . . I don't have the number, Mom. You can get it from information, but there's no reason for you to call me there. . . . All right, I know you'll feel better. Listen, I have to go now, I have to call the agency and leave a message that I'm working an extra day tomorrow. . . . Yes, I suppose I'll get more for overtime. . . . I'll study with Jen all day Sunday, I promise. . . . But you said I could make the decision myself. . . . Okay, okay, I'm not yelling! Arlene is the chaperone, the assistant art director, I'll have her call you. . . . Arlene Saccaro . . . S-A-C-C-A-R-O. . . . I don't know, she's old enough, twenty-five, thirty. . . . About noon tomorrow, maybe later, I'll let you know when I see how long the shoot takes. Look, other people here have to use the phone, too. . . . Okay, bye, Mom."

The slinky jumpsuit dropped to the floor of the dressing area.

"Hey, be careful with that." Amy swept it up and shook it vigorously to keep the creases from setting. "This has to look fresh in the morning."

"Oh, sorry," Kelly said gaily.

Amy gave her a curious look. "Someone's excited about working an extra day tomorrow."

"Is it that obvious?" Kelly bit her lip.

"It's obvious." Amy smiled. "And I know why.

Who could blame you? If a handsome guy like that was interested in me, I'd be excited, too."

Kelly grabbed Amy's arm. "Do you really think he's interested in me? Even after he went out with Cheri last night?"

"It seems that way. Congratulations, I guess the best gal won." Amy wrapped the jumpsuit carefully in a plastic bag and hung it in the closet next to the other costumes. "I have to tell you, Kelly, you're much nicer than most models I work with. You have such a fresh, down-to-earth quality. Don't ever lose it."

"Thanks," Kelly said easily. "I'd better go. I have to meet Arlene downstairs. Are you coming to the hotel?"

"In a while. I have more to do here first. I'll drive over with the crew later, so I guess I won't see you till the morning."

"Okay, see you then. 'Bye."

Humming to herself, Kelly skipped down the stairs. Mickey appeared on the bottom step.

"Mickey! Hi!" Her eyes brightened immediately.

"Hi, yourself, Doc. So what gives? Are you staying out here with the rest of us, or heading for your usual mysterious rendezvous?"

"Oh—that. Actually, I'm staying out here—in the hotel."

He smiled knowingly. "I see. So those special plans you mentioned for tonight have been canceled?"

"Yes, as a matter of fact, they were." It was

true—she didn't have to do her homework. She fingered the smooth wood of the banister. "Um, how about your plans?"

He laughed. "I didn't have anything special on, I just said that to get rid of Fiona. Anyway, my schedule seems to be out of my hands." He paused and stared at her so intently that she became uncomfortable. "So maybe you'll have some time for your patient."

"My patient . . . meaning you?" She felt faint.

Mickey glanced quickly, left and right, over his shoulders. "I don't see anyone else around here with thirteen stitches in his leg. Yeah, I mean me."

The bottom seemed to drop out of Kelly's stomach. "Sure. I'll have plenty of time for you." Her palm was suddenly so clammy her hand slipped off the banister. Mickey stepped close to her and flipped a curl off her forehead.

"Good. I could use a little more tender loving care."

He was so close, she felt dizzy. She struggled to think of something to say to postpone his leaving. "Um, are you driving to the hotel with Arlene?"

"No, I'm supposed to catch a ride with Steve."

"Oh . . . I'm going now. Well, then . . . I guess I'll see you first thing tomorrow."

He grinned his little-boy grin at her, as if she'd said something terribly amusing. "Sure, tomorrow. Arlene's waiting—you'd better get a move on."

"Okay." She looked back at him as she headed toward the front door. "Well, good night."

Mickey waved from the stairs. *"Au revoir."*

Kelly reached for the door. Behind her, she heard Mickey cry out as if someone had stepped on his foot, and she paused, listening.

"Oops, I'm sorry," Maxi's teasing voice rang out. "I didn't see you coming. I was looking the other way."

"You were looking the other way all day," Mickey answered, "but I wasn't—you were magnificent in that jumpsuit."

"Thanks. Maybe you should spend more time looking at the big girls."

"Maybe you should spend more time looking at the big boys," Mickey retorted.

Maxi gave a gay little laugh.

Kelly felt a queer sickness in her stomach as she tugged on the heavy front door. "You were magnificent . . ."—the same word he'd used to describe Kelly earlier! "You should look at the big boys . . ."

Mickey's sly grin and faintly mocking expression seemed to follow her to the car. *So what,* Kelly told herself—*nobody ever said Maxi wasn't beautiful, of course she is. There's nothing wrong with Mickey noticing a beautiful girl and teasing her a little, it's only human. Completely human,* she decided. *There's nothing wrong with that at all.*

The Kendalls slid to one side of the backseat, complaining as usual, as they made room for

Kelly. Cheri shot them an impatient look from her seat in front next to Arlene.

"Isn't Maxi coming?" Kelly asked.

Cheri snorted. "She's hanging around you-know-who."

"Who's that?" Fiona demanded.

"Alex Hawkins, Steve's assistant," Cheri said impatiently. "Where have you been? There's a hot romance going on right under your nose and you don't even notice!"

"It isn't exactly a hot romance," Kelly said indignantly. "It seems pretty one-sided to me. I'm sure Alex isn't really interested. He's just amusing himself while the shoot lasts. Maxi's not Alex's type."

"Uh-oh, I seem to have struck a nerve," Cheri cracked. "It probably isn't serious, you're right—but at least Maxi's only after one guy. Some people around here seem to want every man to themselves." She let out a long, dramatic sigh. "The allure of the young innocent—ha!"

Kelly stiffened. "Cut it out, Cheri. I'm not after Alex. We happen to be good friends and I'm just looking out for his interests. Maxi is obviously a gold-digger."

"Alex seems to know exactly what he's doing," Cheri said, with that same look of amusement Mickey had worn.

"Well, I know what I'm doing, too," she declared.

"Sure you do." Cheri leaned her head against the seat and closed her eyes. "I'm beat. Twelve-hour days are too much for me. A nice hot bath and a good night's sleep are all I want right now."

"That sounds good to me, too," Kelly murmured, as much as she hated to agree with Cheri on anything.

"Sure, a hot bath and a hot night—with Mickey," Cheri yawned.

"I'm not planning a hot night with anyone! Oh, what's the use," Kelly said crossly. "Think what you want, Cheri, it doesn't bother me. I happen to know how to have real relationships with people, and obviously you don't, so I'll just take everything you say as a compliment." She folded her arms across her chest. That should take care of Cheri! But to her chagrin, Cheri had already fallen sound asleep. Her little speech had been wasted.

"There, there," Sir Ernest said, patting Kelly on the knee, "don't worry about your boyfriend. I admire a young lass with a temper."

"Sir Ernest," she said patiently, "watch my lips while I say this: Keep your paws off me!"

Arlene chuckled, and the car sped toward the hotel.

Ten

Cheri dropped her bag on the floor and flopped onto the couch, scowling. "Big deal, a suite— what that really means is one crummy bedroom and this excuse for a living room."

Kelly covered a yawn with one hand. "I'm not thrilled we have to share a bedroom, either, but you don't have to be so nasty about it. This hotel seems pretty nice to me."

"Spare me," Cheri said. "Just because Marilyn and Arlene are rooming together and Amy and Maxi haven't gotten here yet, doesn't mean I enjoy getting Miss Pollyanna as a roommate."

"Knock it off, Cheri. It will be easier for both of us if you try to be pleasant."

"Oh, don't worry about me. I'm taking my bath and going straight to bed. You can have this luxurious suite all to yourself. Hey, are you going to order anything from room service?"

"Suddenly I don't have any appetite," Kelly muttered.

"Suit yourself."

Kelly soon heard water running in the bathtub while Cheri padded back and forth from the bedroom to the bathroom. She glanced at the TV but felt too bored to bother with it. Flopping in a chair, she picked up a magazine instead, and thumbed through it restlessly. All the while, she was wondering if her mother really would call the hotel to check up on her.

How embarrassing. I only hope Cheri doesn't find out. She'd be sure to tell Mickey I'm so young my mother still checks up on me. If only nothing bad happens before tomorrow, I'll have one last chance with Mickey.

When the phone did ring, she jumped up and snatched it off the hook. "Hello?" she grumbled into the phone, sure it was her mother calling.

"Whoa, what's wrong with you?"

"Mickey! I—I thought it was someone else."

"Well, it's not. Listen, I have a taxi waiting outside, and reservations for dinner at The Yankee Clipper in Montauk. Ever been there?"

"No." She'd never even heard of it!

"You'll love it. It's right on the ocean, a fantastic view, good seafood, and dancing. You deserve a little fun after all the hard work we did today."

Kelly hesitated. If she went out now she'd miss

her mother's phone call, and Cheri might answer the phone. On the other hand, Mickey Pines wanted to be alone with her for a romantic evening. "It's pretty late to be going out, isn't it?"

"The night is young. Come on, say yes."

She *was* hungry; after all, they'd only had a skimpy meal during the break, and suddenly, she wasn't very tired, either. "Okay," she said eagerly, "sure, why not. But we can't stay too long."

"Dinner and one dance, I promise. Meet me downstairs in fifteen minutes."

Fifteen minutes—I can put on more makeup, and I have those big dangly earrings in my bag, and a pair of dressy heels, but these jeans! Now's the time for one of those slinky dresses I modeled, not faded blue jeans and this stupid old sweater.

Cautiously, Kelly opened the bedroom door. The room was dim. "Cheri," she called softly, "I'm going to stay up and watch TV for a while."

There was no answer. Cheri must have gone straight from her bath to bed. Holding her breath, Kelly tiptoed into the bedroom, crossed to her side of the room, and pulled down the covers on her bed, arranging the pillows to look as if she were sound asleep with the blankets over her head. Then she carefully closed the door behind her. Cheri hadn't moved an inch.

She did her makeup in the living room mirror, trying to make it as glamorous as possible. It would have to do.

* * *

"You were right, Mickey, this restaurant is magnificent."

As she paused at the entrance to the dining room at The Yankee Clipper arm in arm with Mickey, Kelly realized no one cared how you dressed when you were with a movie star. Every eye was on them as the maître d' showed them to their table—the best in the house, he said, right by the picture windows, commanding a wide view of the ocean outside.

"What a view! I'll always think of you and the ocean together," she sighed. "But I still feel awkward in jeans. I'm sorry I couldn't get more dressed up."

Mickey waved her protest aside. "Who cares? None of these people care. Forget about it. What looks good to eat? I'm starved."

"Care for a cocktail, sir?" The waitress fluttered her eyelashes at Mickey as she gave him his menu.

"Why not? I've had a long, hard day." Mickey ordered a whiskey and water and turned to Kelly. "What'll it be for you?"

The waitress gave her a suspicious look and Kelly panicked. "Nothing for me," she said sweetly. "Drinking causes circles under my eyes, you know, Mickey, and it just ruins my skin. Arlene would know I was out tonight and she'd tell Meg, and I'd really get in trouble. I'm not supposed to party on a job."

Mickey stared at her as if she were crazy. "Are

you serious? Not even one drink? Come on, relax a little. Arlene will never know."

"Really, I can't," Kelly protested. "I'll have a Perrier with a twist," she told the waitress decisively, but she knew she hadn't fooled the woman.

Mickey glanced at her as if he suddenly understood. "Oh, okay, sure, no problem." The waitress left. "Stupid me, I just realized, you're underage, aren't you? How old are you, anyway, nineteen?"

"Yes," Kelly agreed quickly. "Uh, I'm nineteen. Almost twenty."

"I'm sorry, what a blockhead I am. I'll order two at a time and you can drink one of mine."

"No, really, I meant what I said about the alcohol. I'll enjoy myself anyway, believe me." To her relief, he dropped the issue.

They ordered dinner when the waitress returned with their drinks. Kelly asked for the broiled filet of sole, knowing it was low in calories. Mickey, though, didn't seem to care about watching his weight. He asked for the seafood pasta special. When the waitress left the table, Mickey offered Kelly a sip of his drink. She pretended to enjoy the taste of the whiskey, though secretly she wondered how he could like it.

They talked about the shoot while they waited for their meals. But it seemed to Kelly that they'd only begun talking, when their food arrived. The seafood was delicious—she really was hungry! As Mickey and Kelly were finishing their coffee, the band returned after a short break.

"Come on." Mickey held out an arm invitingly. "I need to move."

"Won't dancing hurt your leg?"

"We'll take it slow."

Mickey held her tightly as they danced, and it was all she could do not to close her eyes and float into a fantasy—*Mrs. Mickey Pines . . . Kelly and Mickey Pines announced plans today to costar in a new film . . .*

"I'm having a wonderful time," she murmured. "Everything is perfect: the food, the view, your dancing."

Mickey laughed. "I dance pretty well for a one-legged man, don't I?" He bent her backward and then spun her around, showing off. Kelly was well aware that they were being watched and admired, but it didn't make her at all self-conscious. She was too thrilled by Mickey's attention. Besides, Mickey had a way of making her feel they had the place all to themselves, that no one else mattered.

They danced until the band paused for another break. As they left the dance floor someone snapped a photograph.

"What was that?" Kelly rubbed her eyes to get rid of the white spots suddenly dancing across her vision.

Mickey craned his neck around. "Oh, it's nobody," he said in disappointment. "Just a tourist, but I guess we got enough publicity for one day with *Celebrity* magazine, didn't we?"

Mickey led her back to the table while the spots before her eyes slowly cleared.

"Yes, we did. Mickey," she asked cautiously, "do you like publicity? I mean, you said so much about hating the phony side of show business, about how you liked to be alone."

"And I meant it. Especially when I'm alone with you." He held her hand and leaned over for a kiss.

Flustered, she pulled back. "But we're not alone," she laughed. "We're in a room full of people."

"So what's the matter with that? You and I are alone at this table."

"But it's so public here," she said apologetically. "I'm a very private person, I've always been like that. Don't think I'm cold, it's just that I can't let go very easily in public."

He nodded. "Everything in its place, huh? Don't worry, I'm the soul of discretion. No affection in public." He sipped his drink thoughtfully. "I guess your boyfriend must feel the same way."

Kelly looked up, startled. "Boyfriend?"

"You know, that guy you've been lying to me about."

Kelly's mouth went dry. "I haven't been lying," she said lamely.

"You're not very good at it," he said calmly. "For instance, when I called your room tonight, you thought it was going to be someone else, didn't you?"

Yes—my mother. "Oh, that," she said weakly.

"And all those phony excuses. Did you think I bought that stuff about your family?"

"I guess not."

"Anyone could come up with a better story than that. Look, Kelly, a girl like you must have lots of guys after her. For future reference, you don't have to lie to me about it, okay? It's cool."

"What do you mean, 'it's cool'? You mean, you don't mind if I date another man?"

Mickey shrugged. "Date anyone you like. Why ask me about it?"

She colored. "Well, I, I wasn't exactly asking your permission, I just thought . . ."

"Thought what?" He picked up the check, glanced at it briefly, and took out a credit card. Then he drained off his last drink, and wiped his mouth on the cocktail napkin. "This was a good idea. I'm glad you came tonight."

"Are you?" she asked. "Are you sure you don't wish someone else had come with you?"

"Hey, what's this?" He covered her hand with his own. "What did I say wrong?"

She felt so terrible she could barely speak. "Nothing, I just thought . . . I thought . . ."

"Say it," he commanded. "You should never be afraid of your feelings."

"I just thought, well, that maybe I meant more to you. . . . I thought you were beginning to like me, that maybe, you wouldn't want me to see anyone else." Her cheeks were burning after the confrontation, and she avoided his eyes. "I know that sounds dumb. We barely know each other."

"Kelly," he said softly, "I didn't know you felt that way." He took both her hands and squeezed them tightly. "Come on, let's get out of this place." He signaled for the waitress and handed her the check and his credit card. After he'd signed the receipt, he stood up and nodded to the maître d'. The man hurried over.

"We need a cab."

"Right away, sir."

Moments later, they were speeding back toward the hotel. As soon as the cab let them off in front of the hotel, Mickey put his arms around Kelly and kissed her. Her heart pounded.

"Maybe we'd better go inside," she said.

"That's right, everything in its place."

Kelly tiptoed into the hallway where their rooms were, glancing over her shoulder constantly. "I feel like a criminal."

"What for?"

"They're so strict with models on a job. You're lucky. No one watches you like a hawk. I expect Arlene to pop out any minute. The worst part of modeling is the way you get treated like a baby sometimes."

"No one's going to know what you did."

He tightened his arms around her waist, and she hoped he couldn't hear her heart pounding.

"No one's going to know a thing," he whispered, nuzzling her ear. His breath smelled faintly of alcohol, but it wasn't too unpleasant, and she could hardly pull away after having returned his kiss outside the hotel.

"Nice," he murmured. "But why don't we slip into something more private, like my room." He backed her up to his door.

"Oh, I ought to get some sleep, or I really will have circles under my eyes in the morning."

He slipped his hand inside her parka and rested it on her sweater. "That's what makeup is for, isn't it, to cover the circles? Don't worry about it."

She wanted to move his hand away and tried to think of a polite way to phrase her request. All she could come up with was the line she'd given Sir Ernest, and that would hardly do.

"Come on in, I want another drink." To her relief, he took his hand away to fish through his pockets for his room key.

"Do you need another drink? You had so many already."

"What's with you?" He didn't bother to hide the irritation in his voice.

"Nothing, I—nothing. I guess I'm more tired than I realized."

"Then I guess I'll have to wake you up again." He pulled her toward him, nuzzling her lips, and slowly slid his hands back under her jacket. She was pressed tightly against him.

What am I doing? . . . He's going too far, but how can I tell him to stop?

"Mickey . . . you're going too fast . . . Mickey, wait."

"Wait for what?"

"Kelly! Just what's going on?" Arlene slammed into the hallway.

Kelly nearly leaped out of her skin, but quickly pulled her parka over her disheveled clothes. "Arlene! What are you doing up?"

Mickey groaned and rolled his eyes impatiently.

"I'm waiting for an answer, young lady." Arlene folded her arms and waited grimly.

"Nothing, I'm not doing anything," she said stupidly. "I mean, I was just saying good night. . . ."

"I know what you mean. I'm no fool, Kelly."

"Listen, Arlene, don't be angry. I can explain."

Mickey cut in impatiently. "What is this, the Girl Scouts? We don't have to answer to you."

"I'm sorry, Mickey," Arlene said firmly, "but Kelly *does* have to answer to me. Your private life is none of my business, but Kelly's is when it interferes with her work. And I'm the one responsible for Kelly being in good shape to work tomorrow."

"You're responsible for *me*, too," Mickey said, "and I want you to leave Kelly alone."

"I'd like to do that, Mickey, but I can't." She turned to Kelly angrily. "Did you forget about bedcheck at midnight? Did you think I wouldn't spot your trick with the pillows in your bed?"

Mickey laughed out loud. "Pillows in the bed? I don't believe it. Come on, Arlene, knock off the mother bit and let us alone. We'll be up on time tomorrow." He grabbed Kelly's wrist and started to pull her toward his room, right in front of Arlene!

"Just a minute. Kelly is going straight back to her own room."

Mickey sighed and threw up his hands. "Kelly, you weren't kidding, she thinks you're a baby all right. Look, Arlene, Kelly is old enough to do what she wants."

"Oh, is she? For your information," Arlene said, fuming, "Kelly happens to be—"

"Exhausted!" Kelly yelled before Arlene finished the sentence. "I happen to be exhausted, and I have to get some sleep before the shoot. Mickey, I'm sorry, I'll make this up to you. I promise. Arlene, please, go back to sleep. I'll be fine."

"I'm responsible for you while you're here, Kelly."

"I know that, Arlene, really. I'm on my way to my room now. See?" She gave Mickey an apologetic look. "I'm going now, Arlene, really."

Silently, Kelly tried to communicate a message to Mickey, to say that the embarrassing scene wasn't her fault, but he made an exasperated sound and turned on his heel, disappearing inside his room without a second glance at Kelly. She felt abandoned.

Arlene deposited Kelly in front of her room with a stern warning. "Your mother called me tonight, frantic because nobody answered the phone in your room. I told her you were already asleep, and then I woke up Cheri—she slept right through the phone call, and I had to get the manager to let me in. That's when I found out about your little trick. You'd better remember to act like a professional from now on. It's for your own good."

In the bedroom, Cheri raised her head from the pillow. "How was your big date?" She chuckled slyly.

Kelly exploded. "Does everyone in this entire hotel know what I was doing?"

"Are you kidding?" Cheri said sleepily. "Between Arlene and the manager, I'd be surprised if anyone *didn't* know. I heard Arlene screaming at you—I hope it was worth it." Cheri yawned loudly, then fell back to sleep.

"Of course it was worth it," Kelly said stubbornly.

Three o'clock in the morning. Kelly turned the annoying clock toward the wall. She'd never get enough sleep to be fresh for the reshoot if she kept tossing and turning, feeling absolutely sick about Mickey. If only they'd had more time together.

If I want to straighten things out with Mickey, I'll have to buy myself more time with him tomorrow, enough time to fix this whole mess.

But that would mean breaking her Saturday night date with Eric—Eric, who never pushed her to do things she wasn't ready for; Eric, the boy she'd liked for so long.

I'll see how things go with Mickey tomorrow, she decided. *Then I'll make up my mind what to do.*

Eleven

Cheri appeared in the doorway, her eyes still droopy with sleep. "What time is it? Is it time to leave already?"

Kelly cupped a hand over the phone receiver. "No, Cheri, go back to bed. I had to get up early to make a phone call. We don't go to work until ten o'clock."

"Then why did you wake me up?" Rubbing a fist into her eye, Cheri slammed the bedroom door shut.

Kelly turned back to the telephone.

"Who was that, Kelly?"

"No one important, Mom—my roommate for the night, another model. Anyway, I'm sorry Arlene didn't let me talk to you last night when you called. I guess she knew I was already asleep."

Behind her back, Kelly crossed her fingers. Thank goodness Arlene had covered for her. It wasn't that Arlene thought Kelly was right to sneak out on a date; it was more that she didn't relish dealing with alarmed parents.

"Yes, she said you'd had a hard day."

"We really did, and I'm afraid we're not going to finish early this morning, either. I bet we'll have to work all afternoon." That was unlikely, Kelly knew, but she had to see Mickey and talk to him one more time. After the shoot might be her only chance.

"Oh, no. Kelly, I hope you'll be able to get your schoolwork done."

"I will, tomorrow, don't worry. But, Mom, could you do me a really big favor?"

"I suppose so."

"If Eric calls about our date tonight, could you tell him I'm still stuck out here for the day and I'll call him as soon as I get back to Franklyn?"

"But, honey, when do you think that'll be?"

"I don't know, but I guess it'll be in time to make my date with him," Kelly said cautiously.

"Don't you want to call Eric yourself?"

"No, Mom, I don't have time. Just tell him I have to work all day today." The truth was, she didn't want to talk to Eric until she'd resolved her situation with Mickey. She felt guilty about that—*but after all*, she thought in a burst of

resentment, *Eric won't give up Clarissa for me!
I don't owe him anything!*

"Well, all right." Mrs. Blake sighed.

"Mom . . ." Kelly hesitated. Part of her
wanted to tell her mother everything she was
feeling and to ask what was the right thing to do.

"What is it, honey?"

"Nothing. I'll see you later, okay? 'Bye, Mom."

After she hung up the phone, Kelly tried to go
back to sleep, but she was too keyed up. She lay
awake until it was time to start getting ready for
the final shoot.

After a good night's sleep, everyone else was
more relaxed and eager to finish the shoot.
Models and celebrities alike whizzed through
hair, makeup, and wardrobe. Alex had the equipment set up and the lighting arranged by the
time everyone was ready so that no time would
be wasted.

"Okay everyone, hold it and smile!"

The camera flashed. Steve relaxed and grinned
gratefully at the group assembled again in the observatory. "That's a wrap, people. Good work—I
knew it would only take a couple of hours to get
this shot done right."

He climbed down the tall ladder, telling Alex to
begin packing up.

Kelly sighed in relief. The final shots had been
easy after all; with everyone rested and cheerful,
the party scene had come together with the right

spirit. The only trouble was that Mickey had seemed so sleepy and irritable that Kelly felt even more awkward and embarrassed about the night before.

"I have an announcement to make," Arlene called gaily. "To make up for the unexpected overtime, and to thank you all for being such troupers, we've arranged a little cast party for this afternoon. Come down to the porch when you're out of costume."

There was a bustle of excitement in the room and Amy clapped Kelly on the back. "A party— boy, do I need one! How about you, Kelly?"

Parties after a long shoot were a tradition Kelly usually loved. "It sounds like fun, I guess."

"You don't sound too happy." Amy glanced meaningfully at Mickey. "True love never runs smooth, huh?"

"It's nothing like that," Kelly protested. "I'm a little tired, I guess."

"Sure, that's it," Amy said mildly. "But you'll feel better after you've eaten some lunch, I'm pretty sure."

"Sure, I'm just hungry," Kelly murmured to herself, wishing it were that simple. She tried not to watch as Mickey left the room without glancing her way. He seemed to have forgotten all about the "tender loving care" he'd asked for yesterday.

* * *

Alex was putting the last reflector stand in the hall as Kelly passed by on her way to the upstairs dressing room. He stopped when he saw her, and they exchanged wary looks.

"Have fun last night?" Alex's tone was light, but held a note of challenge, and Kelly bristled.

"I don't see how that's your business. Did I ask what you and Maxi did last night?" She tried to walk past, but Alex caught her arm.

"Kelly, wait. Everyone knows about your scene with Arlene last night."

That Cheri has a big mouth! Kelly thought. "So?" she said. "Is there any law against going out after a hard day of work?"

"No. But what gives, Kelly? You said you couldn't get involved with me because you were true to Eric Powers. Now you're chasing after Mickey Pines like some star-struck kid. I can't figure you out."

Alex had hit on the problem that had kept her awake the night before. *But if Mickey really likes me, I'm not chasing him.* She said defensively, "Eric has nothing to do with this. I can't help it that I met Mickey, and that he likes me."

Alex snorted. "Likes you? He'd like anyone who threw herself at him the way you did."

"That's not true. He could have picked Cheri, or Maxi."

"They eliminated themselves," Alex pointed out. "Besides, they're both tougher than you and can handle it. You're setting yourself up for a fall.

You don't know how to handle someone like Mickey."

"Don't I?" Her temper flared. "You're always saying how naive I am. Well, maybe after Mickey I won't be naive anymore."

Alarmed, Alex tightened his grip on her arm. "What does that mean? I warned you, Kelly, you're getting in over your head."

"Not if Mickey cares for me, I'm not. That's all that matters, isn't it?" She knocked his hand away, furious at his insinuations. "I happen to believe that Mickey could really care about me if I gave him the chance."

"No," Alex said quietly, "you've got that all mixed up. I'm the one who really cares."

She drew in her breath sharply. "If you cared, you wouldn't be hanging around with Maxi."

For a moment they just stared at each other. Alex was the first to drop his eyes.

"Okay, here's the truth. I'm not interested in Maxi; you must've guessed that. She's not for me. I was just angry that you were so impressed with Mickey. I'm not a famous movie star, so how could I compete with him?"

Kelly shrugged helplessly. "I don't know. I don't know why I feel the way I do, Alex, but I can't help it. Mickey is . . . unique. I've never known anyone like him."

"Don't be stupid. He's not sixteen—he expects more from you than some kid like Eric. You think you're going to like playing it his way? Good luck."

"What do you mean, 'playing it his way'?"

"You know what I mean. You think he wants to go on holding hands and sneaking kisses?"

She shifted uneasily. Alex seemed to understand the way she'd felt the night before: she *hadn't* liked playing it Mickey's way.

"I can handle it, Alex."

Alex laughed. "You should see the look on your face. I'm right, aren't I?—you don't like being out of control. I knew you'd see it my way. Well, remember this: it takes courage to admit you've been wrong."

Her eyes blazed. "Then I'm glad you had the courage to admit you were wrong about Maxi!" She tossed her head arrogantly. "Don't worry about me, Alex Hawkins. Some of us know exactly what we're doing!"

Arlene had spared no expense on lunch. The Golden Plate Caterers of Southampton had created an extravaganza of lobster, shrimp, and crabmeat. Platters overflowed with cold salads and fruit, wicker baskets were stuffed with sweet rolls and fresh breads, and the dessert table held so many delicacies that Kelly's mouth watered just looking at them.

As they helped themselves, the cast and crew shared a new feeling of camaraderie. Even the Kendalls seemed to mellow, and for once Cheri forgot to make wisecracks at every opportunity.

"There must be something magic in that food," Lisa remarked to Kelly. "I've never seen this group get along so well. They don't even need Mickey to lighten the mood."

"Yes, but he's doing a good job, anyway," Kelly said, nodding toward the coffee machine where Mickey was charming a small group with endless anecdotes about film stars he'd worked with. But to Kelly, he'd been coldly polite all morning.

Lisa laughed. "He knows so many funny stories, how can anyone resist him?"

Uncomfortable at that thought, Kelly looked out the window. It was a gloomy, overcast day. "That's funny, someone is walking on the beach. I didn't know there were any other houses nearby."

"There aren't really. It must be a hiker."

"He looks familiar," Kelly mused. Then she looked more intently at the distant figure.

"Have you tried the chocolate croissants?" Lisa asked. "They're heavenly."

"No, I . . . oh my gosh!" Kelly gaped in disbelief. "I'll be right back!"

"But where are you going? Oh, well, I'll save you one," Lisa called after Kelly as she dashed from the room.

Grabbing her parka from the wall, Kelly let herself out a side door and kept well away from the sun porch as she ran behind the house.

"Hey, you," she yelled at the solitary hiker. "Over here. Hey! Look up!"

The boy waved, a wide grin spreading over his face, and Kelly motioned for him to meet her by the thick hedges.

"Eric Powers," she yelled, as soon as they

were hidden by the hedges, "what are you doing here!"

"Kelly, I'm so glad you saw me. I didn't know where to look for you, and I wasn't even sure this was the right house."

"This is the right place, all right," she said grimly.

"I knocked on the front door but no one answered."

"I guess we didn't hear you." Nervously, she looked around. They could still be seen from a certain angle. She pulled him against the house. "Uh, it's windy, Eric, let's stand here."

"I called your house and talked to your mom. I felt sorry for you when she said you'd be working all day, so I decided to come out and give you a ride home."

The color drained from Kelly's face. "But . . . but I'm not done yet. Not nearly done. . . . Did you intend to wait here all day?"

"Why not? I wanted to see you. And there's another reason. . . . I—"

From the direction of the mansion came a shout—Alex, calling her name. The last thing she needed now was for Eric and Alex to meet face-to-face!

"Not now, Eric," she said wildly. "Look, I can't talk now, it's a really bad time. I'm very busy with this shot."

"I can wait for you. I'd like to watch you work."

"No, that's a terrible idea—I mean, that's not

such a good idea. We don't allow strangers on the set. They'd be really mad at me. You should head back, and I can meet you in Franklyn, okay?"

Eric stared at her for a moment. "I figured I'd watch very quietly; no one could object to that."

"Yes, they could object," she insisted.

"Come on, let me in, Kelly. This is silly."

Voices sounded behind them from the direction of the hall.

"Let's get this equipment into the van, Alex, then we'll all drive over to the disco," she heard Steve say.

Kelly gasped. "Uh, wait right there, Eric."

She slammed the front door in his face.

"Alex, Alex, I have to talk to you right away—it's urgent!"

"We're loading the van," Alex told her, "and then everybody's going to the disco in Quogue, Hot Tin Roof."

"Everyone? Uh, well, that's great that you're going, Alex. Have a good time."

"Yes, but first, we really do need to talk, Kelly."

"No, we don't! You need to relax, Alex, that's what you need—go right to that disco and stay there and have a great time. We'll talk tomorrow."

"What's with you? I want to get things settled between us before I go anywhere."

"Well, then, at least let's go someplace private . . . the dining room." She hustled him into the room. "Stay right there and don't move—I'll be right back!"

Once again she stepped out the front door. In front of the mansion, Steve was questioning Eric closely. "Not that I'm nosy, but this is private property. Who are you, and what are you doing here?"

Eric colored and Kelly answered swiftly. "It's okay, Steve, he's a friend of mine, Eric Powers. I swear he's not a trespasser, and he was just leaving, anyway."

Behind them, the front door opened and Mickey appeared, flanked by Cheri, Maxi, and Fiona. They made a gay group, joking and laughing loudly.

I am going to have a heart attack and die on the spot! Mickey, Alex, and Eric in one place—how do I get into these spots?

At breakneck speed, she leapt to the front door, wrestled Mickey away from the three women, and practically threw them into the front hall.

"Mickey—don't leave!"

"Get a hold on yourself." He eyed her curiously. "We're not going far, just over to the disco. You could come along if you're interested; everyone's coming."

"I'm not interested—I mean I would be interested, but, uh—there's been a disaster! Something terrible has happened. Steve just told me this minute!"

"Did someone else fall down the dumbwaiter?"

"I'm not kidding. Uh, it's the film, the film of the fifties shots we did in the carriage house. The negatives were damaged and they all have to be reshot. Yes! Steve is getting ready to set up right now. He told me to stop you before you left."

"I thought Steve was going to the disco. Are you sure about this?"

"Absolutely! Go right to the carriage house and wait for me. I'll be right there, okay? Right to the carriage house! No, not out the front door, through the kitchen entrance! It's, uh, much faster."

Mickey shrugged philosophically. "Things sure change fast around here."

Eric was watching Steve load the van when she ran back outside.

"This is it, Kelly. Either we talk right now or I'm leaving," Eric said.

"Eric, this is a very bad time for you to be here. I can't leave now, it's impossible. I'll call you tomorrow . . ."

Steve interrupted. "Kelly, the shoot is over, so don't worry about leaving now. The party was breaking up, anyway, and you don't have to go to the disco with the others. Well, nice meeting you, Eric. I'd chat but I have more work to do."

"Party, what party? I thought you were hard at work."

Kelly looked over Eric's shoulder and blanched—Alex was heading their way, and he didn't look very patient or understanding.

"I thought so," he exclaimed. "I thought you

weren't coming back to get me." He glared at Eric suspiciously. "Who's this?"

"No one," Kelly said, trying to shove Eric to his car.

"No one? I'm Eric Powers." Eric extended a hand to Alex. "Who are you?"

Kelly was getting desperate. Was fate playing some weird joke on her? "Okay, Alex, now you've met Eric Powers, and Eric, you've met Alex Hawkins. Too bad you can't chat but Eric was just leaving, weren't you, Eric?"

"No." Eric set his jaw stubbornly. "I don't believe I was. I came out here to bring my girlfriend home and I'm not leaving without her."

"Girlfriend!" Kelly spluttered. "Since when am I your girlfriend? I thought Clarissa was the girlfriend and I was second best."

"That's not true."

"Well, you never told me!"

"You didn't give me a chance."

"Calm down, kids. Hot tempers never solved problems," Alex said mildly.

Eric ignored him. "All I know is that we have a date for tonight. Why don't you want to go back to New Jersey with me?"

"What? She'd miss the chance to spend some time with a movie star?" Alex raised his eyebrows ironically. "An older, *experienced* movie star."

"Alex, this is none of your business," Kelly said hotly.

"I'm looking out for Eric. We men have to stick together."

"Leave Eric out of this."

"Yeah, I can handle this myself," Eric protested.

"You don't understand," Alex told him. "I'm on your side. I think Kelly should go back with you. It's the only honorable thing to do, under the circumstances."

"Stop it, Alex. Eric, listen to me. I'll be home later, okay? I'll call you."

Eric shook his head, looking from Kelly to Alex. "I think you're both crazy. All I know is that I shouldn't be here. I'm sorry I butted in where I don't belong."

"Oh, Eric, don't go away angry. I can explain."

Alex followed him to his car. "She's right, Eric. Don't go now. Things are just getting interesting around here. A three-way match: you, me, and Mickey Pines. Don't you want to see who wins?"

The blue Toyota roared away.

"Well." Alex smiled brightly. "Eric seems like a nice guy. I'm glad I finally met him after hearing so much about him. Of course, he's not exactly your type. You like a more experienced man, someone worldly and sophisticated—don't you, Kelly?"

"Oh, shut up, Alex."

Twelve

It was quiet and cold in the carriage house. The chrome on the vintage cars gleamed dully as she pushed open the door and stepped inside.

"There's nobody here," Mickey announced. "It's completely empty." He turned in a circle, inspecting the huge garage.

"Is it?" Now that she'd finally gotten him alone, she was at a loss for words.

Mickey, his hands in his pockets, scraped a foot across the damp cement and laughed. "Come on, what's this all about? There isn't any reshoot, is there?"

"No," she admitted. "I made it up. I . . . I had to get a moment alone with you."

"I thought it was something like that." There

was a long pause. "I guess the next move is up to you, Kelly."

She took a deep breath, glanced at him once, then blurted it out. "I just had to talk to you. I couldn't let you go, not after what happened last night. I felt so awful about the way it ended. With Arlene there watching, I had to leave without saying anything. There was so much I wanted to say to you."

"Say it now. I'm listening."

"I can't look at you and say this." She closed her eyes. "You're more wonderful than any boy I've ever known, and I wanted to be with you so much last night. But today you seemed so cold. You didn't spend any time with me at all. I wanted it to be so different, the way it was on the beach, special and private. But today you were ready to leave without saying a word, and I need to know why—I need to know what you think of me."

He smiled. "Is that what we came out here for? To talk? Come on, let's go upstairs; we can use one of the rooms."

"Upstairs? Isn't Steve going to lock up soon?"

"Or we could go back to the hotel—I could get a room there, I guess. But I thought you hated public places." He came close and put his arms around her.

"Oh," she said, startled. Gradually she relaxed in his embrace. "This is nice." She sighed, feeling protected and reassured. "What I'd really like is to take another walk on the beach, like the first day."

"Yeah, yeah, that was nice," he said, picking up a strand of her hair and twisting it playfully. "But it's pretty cold out there, isn't it? And why waste time?"

"It's not a waste of time. It was wonderful, the way you talked to me and told me how you really feel about your life. That's what I want to do today. I want to be with the real Mickey Pines, not the Hollywood image, like you said."

"I said that?" He laughed softly.

"Yes. You told me how you really felt about your work and your relationships. You were so sweet, talking to me. I . . . I really felt close to you."

"You know, Kelly, talking is fine, but sometimes, action is even better." He tightened his arms around her and nuzzled her neck.

"But . . ."

"But what?"

"I don't know. I just . . . I thought we might talk more."

His voice was muffled by her hair. "Look, I don't feel like having a soul-searching discussion right now, okay? I need to relax. Let's just have a little fun."

"Well, okay, sure . . . but, is that all you want?"

"What else is there?"

"Other things," she said, beginning to feel foolish, "like getting closer to each other."

He dropped his arms with an impatient sigh.

"Don't get mad, but I thought you wanted to get to know me better. The real Kelly Blake," she joked. "I thought I was special to you, different from all those phonies you meet."

"You're different all right. But I didn't think you were this different!" His voice rose with annoyance. "And I didn't think you were a tease."

"I'm not a tease," she protested, astonished. "Don't you understand what I'm saying?"

Mickey glanced at his watch, as if he was getting bored.

"Something's different about you, Mickey." She felt insulted. "I don't understand what's happening to us."

"Us?" He laughed, sincerely surprised. "There is no 'us.' Look, Kelly, you're cute and sweet, but there's only so much a guy can take. I've had enough romantic walks on the beach. I've had enough dreamy glances and longing sighs, and I've had enough of your crazy stories. Let's cut the silly games."

"What games?"

"Next time just tell me when you're involved with another man. If I'm in town and you're free and I see you, great. If not, so be it. We're both adults."

She listened with dismay. So much for fantasies of strolling in the moonlight while gossip columnists whispered of their serious romance.

"This isn't what I expected. I thought you felt the same way I did."

"We had some fun, but I don't have time for stalling. Either we get together now, or we don't."

"And then?"

He raised his eyebrows, totally perplexed. "And then, what?"

"I mean, is this weekend all of it? Do you ever intend to see me again?"

"I hadn't really thought about it. I don't make plans too far in advance. I never know where I might be next."

"But I thought—I thought we were starting something together. Something, well, maybe not permanent, but something lasting. Something that could grow."

"I told you, I don't think about the future."

She folded her hands calmly and took a step away from him. "I guess not. I guess it wasn't the same for you as it was for me."

"Don't look so disappointed."

"It's not that I'm disappointed . . . I'm just sorry." *Sorry that I was so naive*, she thought. *Alex was right.*

"Cheer up," he said, "at least now we understand each other."

"Mickey," she said decisively, "I don't think we *do* understand each other. I haven't been playing any kind of games with you. The truth is, I'm not nineteen. I'm a junior in high school and I live in New Jersey with my parents. That's why I couldn't take a ride home with you, that's why I refused dinner at first, and that's why I lied. I didn't want you to find out I'm only sixteen."

"You're sixteen . . ."

"That's right, and I lied to you."

His eyes seemed to be paler than ever. "Well, uh, you're not telling me anything new." He laughed and looked away for a minute. "Sure, did you think I couldn't tell how young you are? I mean, the way you acted . . . of course I knew, I knew all along."

"You did?"

"Of course. What do you think, I fell for a sixteen-year-old? Come on, you know better than that!"

"No, I . . . lots of people think I'm older. I thought you did too . . . I thought you really liked me." She took a step toward him, but Mickey backed away.

"Hang on, now, the joke's over. I'm no cradle robber!"

"Mickey, please, let's at least be friends."

"Friends? That's all I thought we ever were. Hey, did you think I was serious about you? I just thought we were having a little fun, teasing each other, you know."

"But we weren't teasing. You liked me, you told me personal things about yourself, things you'd only tell a friend."

"Sure, a friend, but that's all. Look, I'd never be interested in a high-school kid. That's just the way I talk to women—girls, I mean."

"You mean you lied to me?"

"Look, I didn't mean anything by it. You were flattered, weren't you?"

"Well . . . yes, I was," Kelly said. *I should have paid more attention to my feelings*, she thought. *I saw him flatter and flirt with every woman in sight.*

"Don't take it too hard, I'm a professional actor, remember? Hey, it's too bad about the way it turned out, but let's be honest; I'm no good for you."

"I guess not," she said slowly.

He looked at her a long time. "Things have a way of working out. You wouldn't want me, anyway, believe me. I'm always traveling and never know where I'll be next . . ."

Kelly thought of Alex's words: "It takes courage to admit you've been wrong." Looking up at Mickey, she said, "I guess I wasn't too straight with you, either. I had to watch the way I acted, pretend I was older. . . . It got to be an awful strain."

He reached out, cupping the back of her head in his hand. "Maybe it would have been different if you *were* older."

Impulsively, she hugged him, a friendly hug this time. At first, he seemed startled and kept his arms in the air, but then he gave her a quick hug back. It wasn't the kind of hug he'd given her before, but it wasn't too bad—kind of warm and affectionate.

"Listen, Kelly. I'm sorry if I was rough on you. Sometimes I'm a little pushy, you know . . ."

"You weren't, don't worry about it."

"Yeah. Well." He stood there, suddenly awkward, grinning at her with that little-boy look again, sweet and tough and somewhat abashed.

"Well. I guess I'll go find that disco, maybe get some action."

"Okay." She smiled. "Oh—wait, Mickey, will you do me a favor?"

"What," he asked warily.

"Could you tell Alex something for me? He'll be at the disco with the others."

Mickey relaxed. "Sure, I'll tell him anything you'd like."

"Tell him he was right and I've gone where I belong."

"Where's that?"

"He'll know."

Mickey was in a hurry to leave, but he stopped at the door. "Hey, do you need a ride somewhere? I can't leave you stranded here, can I?"

"I'll call the car service. Don't worry, I'll be fine," she reassured him. "I don't mind waiting."

"Okay then, great." He lingered another moment. "Sixteen." Then he chuckled, saluted, and was gone.

Thirteen

It was hard to believe Mickey was out of her life. Kelly stayed in the carriage house after he'd left, listening to the sounds of cars pulling away. Knowing she had to get back inside to call the limo service before Steve finished locking up, she finally braced herself to reenter the main house.

Alex met her in the front hall.

"Alex! What are *you* doing here?" Kelly demanded. She wasn't looking forward to delivering her message to him in person.

"I had to stay to lock up and set the burglar alarm, but I had to wait until *you* were out of here," Alex retorted.

"I was just going to call the car service." She watched as Alex drew the drapes and checked the locks on the tall windows.

"I can give you a ride home," he said gruffly.

"Aren't you going to the disco?"

"Aren't you, with your dear friend Mickey?"

"No. For your information, Alex, we had a long talk just now, and we decided we're not right for each other."

"Really?" For a moment his eyes lit up in relief. But he quickly recovered his gruff manner. "I could've told you that and saved you a lot of trouble. But I guess you have to learn some things for yourself."

Kelly said firmly, "Alex, one of your problems is that you don't know when to let a subject drop."

He grinned. "Come around with me while I finish locking up, and then I'll take you home."

He took her back out to the carriage house and locked it; then they returned to the main house. Someone had left her bag near the front door, and she grasped it tightly. Alex ushered her out, then slammed and tested the door to make sure it was locked. Lifting a round, metal cover near the door, he inserted a small key and twisted it sharply.

"That resets the burglar alarm. No one could get back inside now without the entire police department knowing about it."

They walked to Alex's car. He opened the door and held it for her. "You know, Kelly, it would make things a lot simpler if you'd just admit I'm the right guy for you."

"Unfortunately, you're the only one who thinks that, Alex."

"I'm not so sure. I think I'm beginning to get to you, Kelly Blake, whether you like it or not."

"You're the last person on earth I'd be interested in."

"Am I? We'll discuss that on the way home."

She slammed the door, making the window rattle, and smiled in satisfaction when Alex winced involuntarily.

"Say good-bye to Windward Point," was all he said before he started the car.

She turned when they stopped at the end of the private drive, for a last look at the mansion. Windward Point would vanish from sight as soon as they joined the main highway.

"If you liked the place that much, I could probably get us invited back again," Alex told her.

"No, thank you," she said in her most cutting tone. "It wouldn't be the same."

"I guess not. As usual, it's been an adventure working with you, Kelly. Never a dull moment. I don't know if I can take another drama like this one."

"You don't have to take anything, so don't worry."

"But I do worry. I worry I'll lose patience before you come to your senses and realize I'm the one for you."

"That's enough, Alex, or I'm getting out of this car right now!" She unlocked the door, her hand poised over the handle.

"Hey, that's dangerous; lock that!" He was

genuinely alarmed, but she'd made her point so she locked the door with a flourish, quite satisfied that she'd had the last word. And in fact, they drove the rest of the long trip in virtual silence. But several blocks from her home, Alex broke the silence.

"What are you going to do about Eric?"

"None of your business."

"I assume that you're going to go to his house, beg his forgiveness for thinking you preferred Mickey Pines, and give him your heart on a silver platter."

Kelly couldn't help laughing. "I sent a message to you by way of Mickey that basically said I was going to do just that."

Alex laughed, too. "You know, Kelly, I hate to say this. But I have a feeling it might work."

As Kelly rang Eric's door bell, she rehearsed her possible excuses again and again. But the moment he answered the door, every excuse fled from her mind.

"Well, aren't you going to say anything, Eric? Not even hello?"

He stared at her mutely. He seemed tense.

"Okay, then you might as well hear the truth, Eric. I acted like a jerk today because I was infatuated with a movie star." She glanced up at him. "I made a big mistake. I admit it, and I deserve anything you say."

To her amazement he seemed to relax once she had admitted the worst.

He nodded slowly. "I thought that was it. You fell for a movie star. I guess that's pretty normal."

"It's normal? That's all you're going to say about it?"

He came out onto the porch, after grabbing a jacket that hung by the door. "Can we take a walk?"

"Sure, if you want to."

Taking her arm he led her from the porch onto the shaded sidewalk. The night air felt pleasantly brisk, and smelled faintly of smoke from the fireplaces in their neighbors' houses.

They walked companionably for a while, and Kelly didn't mind that they weren't talking. Their silence felt comfortable and easy.

"Now I'll tell you the truth," Eric finally said, softly. "The way you treated me today really hurt, and I was angry, too. But I've been doing a lot of thinking about us since then."

"About us?" The words sounded so sweet.

"I drove out to see you today because I was trying to decide about something important, and what happened helped me to decide."

"I remember now, you said you had another reason for coming out, but I didn't give you a chance to explain." They had stepped into the brighter glow cast by a streetlight, and she looked over at him as she spoke. His eyes always seemed so much darker when he was serious—such a beautiful, deep blue.

"The thing I kept asking myself," Eric said, "was why should I expect you to wait for me when I wasn't always there for you?"

"You thought that?"

"Yes. And I realized I haven't been fair to you. I knew you liked me all this time, and I said I liked you, but I wouldn't break off with Clarissa. And you accepted it."

"I didn't mind because I knew you really did like me."

"I know, but I had it easy. Don't you see? In a way, I was using you."

"I didn't think of it that way; I agreed we could both see other people." Feeling uneasy, she released her arm from Eric's and pretended to adjust her scarf.

"But what I did wasn't right," he protested. "It was—well, it was like what you did to me today with that movie star. You figured if I wasn't around then you could go after someone else."

"That's true, I did feel that way. I'm sorry, Eric."

"Don't apologize. I expected you to understand about Clarissa. I guess this afternoon, out at that mansion, I finally realized what it must have been like to be in your shoes."

"Oh, Eric, Mickey didn't really mean anything to me . . ."

He stopped walking and reached awkwardly for her hand. "I made a very important phone call when I got home today. I called Clarissa and broke up with her, for good this time. It's all over between us and she knows it now."

"You broke up with her? For good?" Kelly stopped walking and stared at Eric in amazement.

He laughed softly. "I thought you'd be surprised."

"I just never thought it would really happen."

"But it did happen. Are you glad?"

"Of course I am . . . Oh, Eric. Does this mean neither of us will see other people?"

Eric stared at her in disbelief. "I thought that's what you wanted all along."

"Yes, yes, I did. I guess I still do. I don't know, you really caught me by surprise."

She couldn't help thinking of Alex, and the way he'd looked at the mansion when she'd admitted she wasn't meeting Mickey at the disco. Sure, he'd pretended to be smug and uninterested, but he *had* waited for her to make sure she was all right, and the relief in his eyes had been obvious. . . . But it was ridiculous to be thinking about Alex when she wasn't interested in him romantically. Eric was the one she wanted.

"That *is* what I wanted, Eric. I guess I just have to get used to the idea that I finally have what I wanted."

"I hope that's all it is, because I realized today that I . . . I think I know now that . . . that you mean an awful lot to me. More than I ever realized before."

"Oh, Eric, that's so good to hear."

He put his arms around her and hugged her tightly, and suddenly her hesitation seemed foolish. Eric cared for her; she was sure of that. She kissed him, feeling a burst of happiness.

"Kelly, let's start all over again, fresh, and this time you won't have to worry about any competition. That is, if you want to, if you think you'd be happy with an ordinary guy like me."

"Ordinary? You're not ordinary, Eric. In your own way you're a pretty special guy."

"I'm no movie star."

She looked deeply into his warm blue eyes, and suddenly Mickey Pines or anyone else seemed a pale imitation. Eric was real, and he wanted her.

"You don't have to worry about any movie stars—they aren't all they're cracked up to be. Inside they're only people, just like you and me, and believe me, like us, they can be far from perfect."

"What?" Eric said, smiling. "You're not too far from perfect, you know."

"Oh, Eric," she started to say, but the words were lost as he bent down and touched her lips with his.

ABOUT THE AUTHOR

YVONNE GREENE was born in the Netherlands and emigrated to the United States as a young girl. At seventeen, she began a successful international modeling career, which she still pursues today. She has been featured on the pages of all the major American and European fashion magazines. Ms. Greene is also the author of two best-selling Sweet Dreams novels, *Little Sister* and *Cover Girl*, and *The Sweet Dreams Model's Handbook*.

Kelly Blake
TEEN MODEL

If you enjoyed reading this book, there are many other series published by Bantam Books which you'll love – SWEET DREAMS, SWEET VALLEY HIGH, CAITLIN, WINNERS, COUPLES and SENIORS. With more on the way – SWEPT AWAY and SWEET VALLEY TWINS – how can you resist!

These books are all available at your local bookshop or newsagent, though should you find any difficulty in obtaining the books you would like, you can order direct from the publisher, at the address below. Also, if you would like to know more about the series, or would simply like to tell us what you think of the series, write to:

Kim Prior,
Kelly Blake,
Transworld Publishers Ltd.,
61–63 Uxbridge Road,
Ealing,
London W5 5SA.

To order books, please list the title(s) you would like, and send together with a cheque or postal order made payable to TRANSWORLD PUBLISHERS LTD. Please allow the cost of the book(s) plus postage and packing charges as follows:

All orders up to a total of £5.00   50p
All orders in excess of £5.00   Free

Please note that payment must be made in pounds sterling; other currencies are unacceptable.

(The above applies to readers in the UK and Republic of Ireland only)

If you live in Australia or New Zealand, and would like more information about the series, please write to:

Sally Porter,
Kelly Blake,
Transworld Publishers (Aust) Pty Ltd.,
15–23 Helles Avenue,
Moorebank,
N.S.W. 2170,
AUSTRALIA

Kiri Martin,
Kelly Blake,
c/o Corgi and Bantam Books New Zealand,
Cnr. Moselle and Waipareira Avenues,
Henderson,
Auckland,
NEW ZEALAND

TRUE LOVE! CRUSHES! BREAKUPS! MAKEUPS!

Find out what it's like to be a COUPLE.

Ask your bookseller for any titles you have missed:

Coming soon . . .

COUPLES SPECIAL EDITION
SUMMER HEAT!

SWEET VALLEY HIGH

Tell your kid sister, your sister's friends and your friend's sisters . . . Now they can all read about Jessica and Elizabeth in SWEET VALLEY TWINS – a brand new series written just for them.

You love reading about the Wakefield twins, and the whole gang at SWEET VALLEY HIGH. You love the real-life thrills and tender romance on every page of every SWEET VALLEY HIGH book. Now there's something new and exciting – it's Francine Pascal's latest series – SWEET VALLEY TWINS. These are the stories about Jessica and Elizabeth when they are just twelve years old, as all the Sweet Valley excitement begins.

SO PASS IT ON!

SWEET VALLEY TWINS is coming soon!

BEST FRIEND No. 1
TEACHER'S PET No. 2 – Both available in June 1987